D1526854

Screwed Pooch
a novel by Jan Millsapps

To Jo Ann -
I hope you [enjoy] this
enjoy book!
JM

ISBN: 978-1-4196-7070-1
LCCN: 2007905026

Publisher:
BookSurge Publishing
Charleston, SC
www.booksurge.com

Cover design by Jan Millsapps. Vintage trading card used with permission of The Topps Company, Inc.

Printed in the United States of America

Screwed Pooch

a novel by Jan Millsapps

To my parents Ruby and Woodrow, who trained me, fed me treats, brought me inside when it rained, lavished their love on me, and allowed me to go off leash as soon as I was able.

— JM

Laika, a.k.a. Kudryavka, wearing her travel harness. Her spacecraft is behind her. (Photo: private collection)

Contents

Preface

"Gaps," writes video artist Bill Viola, "become most interesting as places of shadow, open to projection."

It was the gaps — and possibilities for illuminating them — that drew me into the story that has become *Screwed Pooch*.

We know little about the first space explorer; many facts surrounding Laika's selection, training and launch are difficult or impossible to find, and conflicting stories abound. She and her spacecraft are mis-identified in many photos. Varying accounts have been offered about her name, breed, gender, origin and eventual fate.

Most likely she was a stray mongrel grabbed from the Moscow streets and hurriedly trained for her historic mission. Her name was Kudryavka, but once in space, she became "Laika," Russian for "barker," but also the name of a Samoyed breed. She has been identified as huskie, beagle, terrier and mongrel. She was small, only 6 kg (13 lbs) and about three years old when she was launched into sudden global prominence aboard Sputnik 2, where she lasted from a few hours to a week and a half, depending on which account you read.

Screwed Pooch is fiction based on facts the historian in me has uncovered and the storyteller in me has interpolated, retouched and augmented to create a narrative spanning the few crazed weeks between the launch of Sputnik 1 (the first artificial satellite) on October 4, 1957, and Sputnik 2, a hastily assembled spacecraft carrying the first space passenger, on November 3.

My goal has been to find and reveal the personalities — both human and canine — that came together to initiate space exploration. While I have tried to maintain the historical integrity of real-life characters like chief designer Sergei Korolev and Laika's trainer, Oleg Gazenko, I've used actual facts to add depth to their personalities: Korolev's uncompromising drive to succeed as fueled by his near-death gulag experience, and Gazenko's deep affection for his dogs jeopardizing the mission he knew would kill one of them.

I have tried to invent plausible encounters between historical figures and fictional characters, working especially hard to provide female voices so often absent from history. There were female photographers working in Soviet media; I read about one named Galina at Novosti and the name stuck. Later I was amazed to find a photo of Oleg Gazenko with two space dogs at a press conference — crouching below them is a curly-haired woman, the Galina in my story. I've seen photos of numerous young women who worked at the Institute where the space dogs were trained. Korinna is a blend of many of these, but I borrowed her thick eyeglasses and frizzy hair from another historical photo — of a young Hillary Rodham. The priest is easy to peg; he's a mix of his designated hero Jesus and the American cowboy Hopalong Cassidy.

My inspiration for Laika's neighborhood came from a fake "main street" on a movie back lot at my son's film school; the character Lilia began as a pretty manikin gazing from a second floor window, just above a fake Krispy

Kreme donut shop, which morphed into her husband Victor's bakery.

Finally, I have tried to develop the canine characters as key players in the international space race. Laika provides the missing "reverse angle" to official accounts of her incredible journey by adding vital first-person commentary. She's the spirit and history of female endeavor as carried on by the likes of Sacajawea, Harriett Tubman, and Amelia Earhart. She's also me, of course, and countless brave women I've known — my mother and my aunts, my sister, nieces and grandmothers, female friends both animal and human.

Dogs are not human; a feminist dog may not exist. Yet research suggests our canine counterparts may be more sentient than we think, one reason the Soviets chose dogs as early mission stand-ins for themselves. Females were used almost exclusively; this was a simple matter of bathroom logistics.

I borrowed the title *Screwed Pooch* from American slang originating during World War II; to "screw the pooch" meant messing up badly, a phrase used frequently in the early space program, when rockets exploded, stages refused to separate, personalities collided with the demands of a society bent on global dominance, and pesky human emotions intervened at the most inopportune times.

The Soviets, far more than the Americans, kept their "screwed pooch" disasters secret. Soviet space history is notoriously marked by gaps: unsuccessful missions never happened; out-of-favor cosmonauts suddenly disappeared from retouched photos; the identity of the brilliant "chief designer" was a carefully guarded state secret until after his death.

While the incompleteness of history may frustrate anyone trying to gain a total understanding based on the facts alone, the very same gaps can prime the imagination with rich potential for creative discovery and interpretation of a story that may never be fully known. Until the story is composed, until the historical narrative glue is applied, we cannot know fully what history is trying to tell us. Until we reflect on history from our current perspective, we may not understand its relevance for our present time.

There's one more reason we must locate and illuminate the screwed pooch gaps in all our histories. Out of the very worst predicaments can come the very best we have to offer. When resourceful victims manage to overcome certain disaster, a transcendent moment is created, one that can be shared by individuals and communities in the past and present, and in all parts of the world.

That is why the Moscow Animal Shelter has chosen Laika as its enduring symbol, as a mascot of hope rather than exploitation, and that is why I have made her the heroine of my story.

Jan Millsapps
San Francisco
June 2007

Introduction

My entire existence adds up to this:

Three years on the streets, a few hours in space, and an eternity in dog heaven — half a century so far and I'm having the time of my afterlife. In retrospect, my time on Earth was lonely, uncomfortable, and frightening — but fortunately brief. It was the part in-between — getting from there to here — I still have nightmares about. It was a stern lesson in how horrible things can get, and how glorious, all at the same time: tragedy and transcendence spinning circles around the Earth at 28,000 kilometers an hour.

You've probably heard of me, by one name or another. The Americans, predictably critical, called me "Muttnik," while the Soviets eventually settled on "Laika" — that means "barker" in Russian. Before that, they'd called me Kudryavka — Little Curly — absurdly inappropriate; there was nothing curly about me. I wasn't much of a barker, either; I knew from past experience that complaining out loud never got me anything. Besides, by the time I realized how much trouble I was in, it was too late to make noise.

Maybe my picture showed up in your *Weekly Reader* at school. Or you heard Walter Cronkite on television reporting the launch of Sputnik 2, which caught the Americans off-guard even more than Sputnik 1, because this time a living being was on board. That was me: Laika the space dog. My career was short. I was the only living creature ever sent into space without a re-entry plan. My mission was a suicide mission, only no one asked my permission. I was volunteered, as they say, by the very one I'd fallen in love with, so madly and so completely that the untold tortures he inflicted were tender caresses, the orders he barked were whispered endearments, and, in my lovesick mind, the locks and cages in which he imprisoned me offered absolute proof of my unspeakable value to him. Up until the very end I believed he would protect me, and moreover, that he would return my love in full.

What a gullible pooch I turned out to be! For years I was too embarrassed to admit this, suffering my eventual fate in silence as I watched my own body accelerate in gradual free fall, incinerate and burn into nothingness. All physical traces were destroyed upon re-entry, just as they'd intended, although my spirit survived, and even to this day, my mind is sharp and my memories vivid.

On Earth, government documents and news accounts (often one and the same) could be nursed into any truth deemed necessary. The Soviets were masters at manipulating their stories, and my story required careful, top-secret finessing. While the love of my short life was allowed to grow old as a revered medical scientist, I passed quickly into history as one of his few failed experiments, a blemish soon airbrushed into a rousing success for the Soviet Union: the brave little dog who gave up her life but paved the way for human space flight. Did Yuri Gagarin ever thank me for my efforts on his behalf? Or Gherman Titov? Or Alan Shepherd? I think not. Humans are not normally inclined toward such generosities.

Do I sound bitter after all these years? Yes, because now I know everything. I know my death could easily have been prevented if everyone had just slowed down and done things properly. I know it's not all my beloved's fault, either. His orders came from another human, who was running scared for his own good reasons, and that human's orders came from the absolute worst place — the very top.

That's where we should start.

Part One

Recruitment

1.
Moscow
October 10, 1957

A sparkling chandelier hovers flying-saucer-like above the dignified gathering. Women in formal gowns, diamond necklaces and tall sculpted hair float on the arms of men in somber uniforms generously decorated with flashy medals and epaulets. Vodka flows; the rotund host works the well-mannered crowd, hugging, toasting, laughing uproariously, then condemning me to an early death for no good reason.

Of course I knew nothing about the fancy party. I'd just awakened, ravenous as usual. It was an early autumn evening, a chill just beginning to creep into the unsettled air. I stood and stretched, one hind leg at a time. I had to start moving and keep moving — this was necessary for survival. Hugging the shadows, I hurried along the alleyway, alert to any danger, excitement, or to the smell of food — always a pleasure. In retrospect, if my fate hadn't been sealed during that evening's festivities, I'd most likely have died young anyhow. Everyone said I was fortunate to have survived so far — three years on the treacherous Moscow streets. But they also admitted I was strong and smart; that's why I was still alive, they reasoned, and somehow that made me a good choice for their sudden, crazed plan.

Up until the time they "recruited" me, this was my daily routine: Find food. Find a place to sleep. Stay out of trouble. Usually I ended up at the church around the corner. The young priest with skinny legs and a ruddy complexion was a friend of mine and if he had food to spare, he was always generous about sharing. Tonight he'd already put a tiny sliver of veal and a slightly thicker slice of ham just outside the rear rectory door. I was never inclined toward his religion — too many rules — but I did adore that priest. He was the only human who ever made me feel OK about humanity. I'd peeked under his robes once — that's how I knew about his skinny legs. And that he didn't wear undergarments.

He'd tried to touch me — on my left ear — and I'd bit him. I couldn't help it; contact meant danger and I reacted instinctively. He jerked away; I saw the sorrow in his eyes and felt really bad, even though it was only a tiny nip and the bleeding stopped within minutes. I don't think he'd meant to hurt me, but now I'd hurt him. He pulled a clean handkerchief from the pocket of his robe to wrap his injury, and we left it there, the priest and I. He never tried again and I never apologized for what I'd done.

If the priest who fed me was a good human — and I say he was — then the host of that fancy party was very bad. I don't know if American humans were any better; I never met any Americans. Khrushchev, the man who threw the party, hatched his deadly plan that night to stroke his own patriotic fervor and to feed his insatiable ego. Though short in statue, he'd managed to elevate himself just a few months earlier, becoming sole leader of the Soviet Union; no doubt this sudden vertical move had left him a bit giddy with power.

From bits of information I gathered during what were to be the last few weeks of my life, I learned about this contest between the Soviets and Americans: the "space race." Last week we'd grabbed an early lead, launching Sputnik, a silver ball with four long whiskers, into outer space. All it did was circle the Earth over and over, beeping incessantly, but it scared the stuffing out of folks in the United States, who thought perhaps it was armed, if not with weapons, then with spy cameras to photograph whatever unassuming Americans were up to when it passed overhead every hour and a half.

You'd think our leader would have been bursting with pride over this unprecedented scientific achievement, but on the night of October 4, just after Sputnik was launched, Khrushchev went to bed unimpressed. When he was awakened early the next morning with surprising news from afar — that the Americans, the British and others had reacted with astonishment and concern — Khrushchev realized that the value of the little silver contraption orbiting up above was not what it could do (which was very little), but what the rest of the world feared it might be capable of doing. If the Soviets had developed a missile powerful enough to send this Sputnik into orbit high above the Earth, the same missiles could be loaded with warheads and more Sputniks could be sent into orbit, armed and ready to annihilate earthlings any time, any place. Overnight, worldwide reaction to the news of Sputnik's launch had provided the Soviets with a sudden upsurge in power and an unanticipated propaganda windfall.

That's why Khrushchev threw this private party just a few days later — to gloat and celebrate with all the rocket scientists and military brass. He entertained his guests with amusing tales of American incompetence, about their embarrassingly named "Vanguard," a missile that had not yet gotten off the launch pad. About their president, a bald old soldier who knew little about leading a powerful nation because he'd suggested a joint venture into space (true leaders never offer to share power), and because he'd responded to the news that the Soviets had put "one small ball in the air" by saying their achievement did not concern him "one iota." Although these words did not translate well into Russian (someone suggested it meant the American leader had small genitals), the remark made its rounds among the party guests, who found it hilarious.

After a few more drinks, the host decided a second trip into outer space must be made right away, because some kind of national holiday was coming. Don't ever make public announcements while drinking; nothing good ever comes of it. But this man Khrushchev was so important that whatever he said, drunk or sober, got done.

He grabbed the arm of one of the more prominent guests, The Chief Designer, congratulated him on the success of Sputnik, then lifted his glass and stage-whispered loud enough for everyone to hear, "And now, Mr. Chief Designer, please launch something new into space for the next anniversary of our revolution!"

The partiers tilted their own glasses upward, cheered and applauded enthusiastically, and word quickly spread throughout the gathering that a new spaceship would be built and sent into space — in a mere matter of weeks!

Whispered conversations among The Chief Designer and his associates at the party continued to flow, as did the vodka. Of course plans were already underway to launch another Sputnik, much larger and more sophisticated, just not so soon. Clearly, The Chief Designer would have to put aside his own Sputnik plans to please the boss. A quick new design would be necessary, one that could meet the impossible deadline Khrushchev had just imposed, but also one that would offer the rest of the world yet another startling come-uppance. Someone must have reminded The Chief Designer about the "rocket dogs" who'd been sent aloft in low-altitude missiles, then retrieved and studied to determine the effects of confinement, acceleration and weightlessness. The logical next step of sending a dog into outer space could serve as a valuable scientific experiment if humans were to travel there some day. The Americans were far from prepared to launch any living creature into space. This could be another first for us, another victory — just what the Soviet leader had asked for!

"Space dog," enthused revelers murmured in awe as the drunken evening wore on. Shiny brass buttons near the tight waists of the men's military uniforms were undone, bellies loosed and postures relaxed; perfectly arranged updos on the women showed signs of coming unraveled and red lipstick migrated from their mouths to the rims of their cocktail glasses. Tight conversational groups scattered as lingering guests began sitting quietly apart in ones and twos. The string quartet providing sweet background music all evening could be heard clearly at last.

"We should go," The Chief Designer whispered into his wife's ear. She nodded and hurried to retrieve their overcoats while he began making the necessary, formal rounds of farewell: bear hugs, cheek kisses and mutual promises to celebrate the glory of the Soviet Union again very soon.

An official meeting between Khrushchev and The Chief Designer would be necessary before beginning work on this daring new space mission, but tonight's partiers dispersed, confident that a bold decision had been made: the first living creature would be sent into outer space, a dog.

Indeed, that puppy turned out to be me. Oblivious to the fact that my days on Earth were numbered, I finished my meager but tasty meal and curled up inside a cardboard box in back of the church, where the bitter Moscow wind wouldn't find me. I rushed into a sound sleep sprinkled with pleasant dreams, determined to remain where I was until dawn.

2.

The Chief Designer, the human in charge of getting the Soviets into outer space, had a real name, but for security reasons, the government insisted that it be kept secret; he could not reveal his identity, could not wear his medals or comment publicly on his official activities. When working at the top-secret launch site, he was known only by his code name, "Number 20."

I never understood why the Soviets chose to recognize some lives while steadfastly denying others: I'd soon achieve celebrity dog status, for instance, but this brilliant man's hard work would never be credited during his lifetime and the world would not know his name until after he was dead. My face would appear in *Pravda*, *The New York Times*, *Life Magazine*, even on postage stamps, and my bark would be heard around the world, while the man most responsible for my high visibility would himself remain invisible. I'm not complaining about my own brief moment in the spotlight — most dogs live and die without achieving any glory whatsoever — but The Chief Designer deserved better.

Of course he wasn't happy to hear Khrushchev mouthing off about going into space again so soon, but he was smart enough to keep his own mouth shut. He certainly didn't want to go back to the gulag where he'd spent several miserable years during the Stalin purge; his jaw had been broken and he still had trouble chewing his food — a daily reminder of his past. That's why he responded to the Soviet leader that night with a wide smile and later told his associates that the brief interval he spent between Sputnik 1 and what would soon become Sputnik 2 was "the happiest time of his life."

While outwardly pretending to relish the remainder of the festive evening, The Chief Designer's mind was racing. He could adapt the canine travel compartment used for the low altitude rocket launches, adding the life support systems necessary for a longer trip. He could assemble a simple framework to hold the instrumentation from the first Sputnik's spare parts. When the first satellite was being designed and built, he'd taken time to construct two identical objects, one to launch and one for backup, demanding exacting standards for both — no shortcuts, no rough edges — because he'd assumed the spare would end up as a museum display. Now that the backup was to be the next satellite itself, saving him critical R&D time, he thanked whatever instincts had insisted that the second spacecraft be built as carefully as the first. His biggest challenge now would be combining the canine carrier with the Sputnik and adding enough boost to the launch missile to insure that the heavier payload would reach orbit.

Mentally counting the days until launch, he realized he didn't have time for a separate design process — this new spaceship would have to be designed and constructed all at once. The engineers, carpenters, metalsmiths and electricians would have to move into the uncomfortable warehouse where the designers worked, cramped and cold, for the next few weeks. He'd given his entire staff time off for a well-deserved vacation; now he'd have to call them back to work tomorrow and they'd all have to work without rest until the job was completed. There would be no time for testing or finessing; the first draft would be the final draft, and it would have to work. That's why, if another partier had observed him carefully as the evening wore on, the concern collecting behind his face — and the renewed determination — would have become apparent.

Just after midnight, The Chief Designer and his wife Nina traveled a short distance from the Kremlin to their well-appointed home. He took off his dress uniform, hung it in his wardrobe, rolled up his shirt sleeves, sat down at his broad wooden desk, sharpened a pencil and went to work, sketching new plans and figures, straining to imagine them as realities so soon.

"Aren't you coming to bed?" his wife called to him.

When he didn't answer, she walked into his study and tapped him on the shoulder. He jerked around to face her with an expression she'd seen before, his sorrowful eyes focused far away — in the Siberian prison camp where he'd nearly perished. Nina retreated without another word and slept alone that night and the every night for the next few weeks. Her life, like his, like mine, had been upended earlier that evening by the host's inebriated speech. Maybe that's why The Chief Designer was never much of a drinker; even at the desolate launch site, where alcohol was the only nicety, even after a successful missile launch and the celebratory champagne, he was known as a stalwart tee-totaler.

"So much more must still be done," he'd say with a grim smile; his workers never knew whether he was referring to the current mission, to the next one, or to the one after that.

He'd promised to take his beloved Nina on a rare vacation — to Sochi, a lovely village on the Black Sea. He hoped she'd forgive him; she'd already told her friends about their trip, he was sure. He wondered if she hated him because she was forced to lie about his job, and then to lie about her lies when circumstances forced him to change their plans. What would she say? My husband cannot get away from work. His job is very demanding. If he truly cared about you, her friends would point out, he'd make sure you two could take this vacation together. What kind of a husband is this? What kind of job could cause a man to treat his wife so badly? Sadly, Nina was not allowed to provide honest answers to such reasonable inquiries.

A little past 2 a.m., Sergei Pavlovich Korolev, the secret man with troubled eyes, the dedicated, hard-working and well-behaved Chief Designer of the Soviet space program, put his head in his hands and mourned his own success.

3.

The dead of night and I'm busy admiring myself in the reflecting glass of the church entryway, where I'd hidden in an alcove until all the humans had gone away. Pressing my warm black nose against the cool glass surface, I inspect the narrow white stripe adorning my face, perfectly centered between my big dark eyes. The rest of my face, and my ears, are also dark, so the white contrasts nicely. From the neck down I'm mostly white and runway-model thin — all street dogs are. I back up and turn part way around to check on my high white tail, curving elegantly above my rear end. Everything about me is just as it should be.

A sudden chill interrupted, spiking the fur along my back, but I was nowhere near ready to wake up — it was still dark out — so I ignored it, rousing myself only enough to turn around twice, then resettling in my box, eyes closed, preparing to re-enter to the warm church vestibule in my dream, when I sensed a low insistent roar pushing itself into my ears. Irritated, I shook my head to clear it, but the roar intensified and I realized it was coming closer. I jerked my eyes open just in time to see the blazing lights of an enormous black sedan turning the corner into my street and stopping, though its headlights stayed on and the engine kept idling. A tall, gangly man in an overcoat emerged; I identified his offering by scent more than sight: a potent slab of beef he was pulling from a paper bag with one gloved hand.

Street dogs make poor decisions whenever food is involved, simply because a full stomach always seems the best choice. I was about to make a terrible decision — one that would not only change my life, but would soon end it — just to satisfy my craving for a midnight snack.

I'd already emerged from my box, nose quivering and mind racing; of course I should grab this unexpected treat before me, but my instincts cautioned me to protect myself, so I crept backwards into the shadows instead of lunging for the meat, but it was too late. He'd spotted me — my white coat had given me away. Patiently he cleared his throat and spoke in a low gravelly voice, without emotion.

"Here, you sorry looking bitch."

He was mistaken about my looks, a sure sign he should not be trusted. I lowered my stomach almost to the pavement, flattened my ears, and growled a short warning, but continued sniffing the air in front of me. He wiggled the meat; the scent was mesmerizing. Still, I held back. I thought of the neighborhood priest, of what he might be able to offer me, but I knew his gifts were iffy at best. His own rewards were dependent on the generosity of his parishioners. Sometimes he went to bed cold and hungry like me, gathering his woolen robe tightly around him and earnestly praying for a better tomorrow.

The stranger bent even lower to the sidewalk, his overcoat grazing the pavement, dangling the savory red meat right in front of my face. Try as I might to ignore his offering, I found myself creeping forward. I jumped on the meat and devoured it. He fed me several more pieces and then I began to feel dizzy. I saw him closing in. The last thing I remember seeing was a set of perfect white teeth topped by a bristly dark mustache. Then a net descended over me and I was caught. He laughed out loud as he scooped me up and dumped me into a cardboard box reeking of motor oil. I heard my rear end thud when I landed, then everything was dark for a long time and there were no more dreams.

4.

Dr. Oleg Gazenko had trained the government's low-flying rocket dogs, but now he'd been assigned a higher mission — to locate and train potential space dogs. Small strays were perfect recruits — lean and hardy from life on the streets, plus they were plentiful *and* they were anonymous. No one would notice when a stray dog vanished overnight — or so he thought as he drove away with his fresh catch.

"Did you hear something?" The plump woman sat up beside her snoring husband, pulling at her hairnet, which had slipped to one side, and at her white flannel gown, which had ridden up above her waist as she'd slept.

"What is it now?" The man was not happy to be awakened; he had to start work in his downstairs bakery at dawn: preparing sumptuous tarts, muffins and coffeecakes. Even so, he groped hopefully at her genitals.

"Downstairs, someone in the street." Gently, she pushed his hand away.

Lilia roused her husband Victor often from fear of suspicious activity down below their second story apartment. She couldn't help it; she'd heard these noises before: car doors, footsteps, hushed voices. She imagined uniformed men with weapons pounding on the downstairs door, and if there were no answer, breaking windows and jimmying locks, hurrying up the stairs to where she and her husband slept. People could be arrested on the flimsiest of charges; it only took two complaints by other citizens; you'd be taken away and never seen again. Stalin was not long dead and the horrors of his police state were still within the memory of most citizens; history had taught that no one should be trusted.

"Again, noise in the street?" Victor was cross at being disturbed for no good reason. Sex, apparently, was not on the bedroom horizon.

He slapped his wife hard across her cheek. She gasped for breath and felt the hot imprint of his hand on her face.

"Leave me alone now," he ordered, then turned away from her and went back to sleep.

The dazed woman held herself perfectly still until his snoring resumed, then crept out of bed, careful not to awaken her sister sleeping in the living room. Lilia sat by the kitchen window for the rest of the night, nervously scanning the empty street below for any sign of danger. A single streetlamp stood sentry; not even one car or pedestrian interrupted the warm circle of light it cast on the street and sidewalk.

Near dawn another light appeared, the one people called Sputnik, a tiny pinpoint creeping across the sky overhead, backlit by the rising sun. But Lilia's thoughts were earthbound; she did not look up.

Victor soon awakened and hurried to plant a gentle kiss on the same cheek he'd attacked during the night.

He wrapped his wife in his burly arms and murmured through her hairnet and into her ear how much he loved her, then dressed quickly and went whistling down the steps to another workday; he'd already forgotten his recent brutality.

As soon as he'd left, Lilia turned on the radio, pleased to find a Rachmaninoff symphony she'd use to mask her husband's sounds in the bakery downstairs. The housework could wait; she sat for a while longer in the kitchen window, listening to the complicated music and watching the sunlight chase shadows from the street below. Her husband had never been so angry that he'd hurt her, and Lilia puzzled on what she might have done to incur such wrath. Perhaps her refusal of lovemaking, but this was easy to repair. She'd never say no to him again, she decided, relieved to have solved this embarrassing marital problem with a little early morning soul-searching. She hoped her sister had not overheard what Victor had said and done to her. The walls in their building were wafer-thin and secrets were hard to keep.

Just as she left her seat by the window, preparing to make the bed and clean the kitchen, she realized something was missing: the little stray dog that sniffed her way up and down the street about this time each morning.

5.

I woke up feeling thick-headed and stupid; I'd been drugged and captured. When I slowly raised my head to look around, I realized I was not alone; a row of cages held others who had arrived before me. Most were busy sniffing the air, trying to figure me out. One whined a greeting I chose to ignore; I was not in the mood for small talk.

"What's your name?" one of them persisted. I had to admit that I didn't have one.

"That's OK," another one replied; later I'd learn to call her Albina. "They are very good here about giving out names."

I barked back at her that I didn't want a name so much as I wanted to be let out of this cage. Didn't the others understand we were trapped? Didn't they miss their freedom? But when I asked them, they just wagged their silly tails and behaved as if they'd never heard the word.

Like most dogs that run free, I'd been happy enough in my own little world. I'd known my street intimately; I'd covered every inch of it on a daily basis. Whether by chance or by my own design, I'd always lived alone. Other dogs came around from time to time, but usually disappeared once they'd met me. I liked to think I'd gained a reputation as a tough dog, unwilling to share the limited resources of this neighborhood, but the actual fact was that I had a loathsome personality, and it showed.

Occasionally a boy dog would show up and decide to stay, following me around, sniffing my private parts, climbing on top of me and trying to hump me to death. I'd snarl and growl and eventually shake him off and chase him away. I'd have to spend the next few hours licking myself clean again and carefully re-marking my territory — the puny tree that never had leaves on its branches, the narrow wooden bench, the short fire hydrant, the tall corner light pole. Once, I'd wedged myself behind a loose board in the alleyway to birth my babies; they were all dead before I could clean and feed them. I mourned them briefly — any mother would — but then convinced myself to get over it; I'd have made a terrible parent anyway.

Besides the rectory entrance to the church just around the corner, only two doors opened into my street. The one with the striped awning led to a bakery where a man in a white apron made the cakes, pies and tarts that rested beneath a glass counter. Customers came and went all day long, but were more numerous early in the morning, when the heavenly smells of his fresh-baked muffins spilled from the doorway into the street.

Of course I'd wagged my tail in his direction, feigning friendliness — nourishment could result from this — but the shopkeeper was not fond of animals. Anytime I dawdled outside, he ran out yelling with a broom and chased me away.

The second door led to a dimly lit office where a man dressed in a crisp dark suit sat behind a massive desk, scribbling notes, stopping, leaning back in his chair to stare at the ceiling (I saw nothing there to look at), then returning to his work. His infrequent customers arrived one at a time, took a seat across from him and spent entirely too much time explaining why they'd come. I could tell they were talking too long because I'd see his left foot, hidden under the desk, begin to tap, slowly at first, then more quickly, soon joined by his right foot, in a crazed little rhythm only he and I were aware of.

Soon he'd interrupt. His feet would stop and he'd place both hands palms down on the desk, fingers splayed. He'd speak earnestly, sometimes picking up his fountain pen to write notes as he spoke; soon he'd stand, shake hands with his visitor and walk around his desk to make sure the visitor departed.

When he was alone again, he'd scribble a bit more, then lock his papers inside a desk drawer, using a shiny key he kept in his coat pocket. Sometimes his face would relax into a soft troubled frown, his deep-set eyes clouding over, his right hand unknowingly toying with the small goatee he'd recently grown. Once, when his door was open, I heard him grunt and sigh in obvious distress. I hurried to his threshold, responding with comforting sounds of my own, but he pretended not to notice.

How I longed to wander down my street right now, smelling the treats the shopkeeper was preparing, whining for food and attention outside the rectory door. I'd even welcome the cross words the shopkeeper would have for me or the way the man in his office would ignore me. I yearned to sniff the fire hydrant by the curb, to find out whether another dog had ventured into my neighborhood overnight; if so, I'd leave a pungent message: *don't come back here; this is my territory.*

Was my territory, I corrected myself, looking past the bars of my cage at my new neighbors, gossiping and frolicking in their miserable captivity. They were idiots; I vowed never to become one of them. I'd find a way to get myself out of here and go back home, where life made sense. What was the point, anyway, of just sitting in a cage all day long?

"I'll be gone before you know it," I announced out loud; they grinned and whined, not listening to a word I'd said.

6.

Lilia had often watched the little dog from the upstairs window of the apartment where she and her husband Victor lived, above the bakery. The dog would trot cautiously down the street, stopping frequently to sniff; sometimes she'd squat and pee, then she'd move on. Lilia decided she'd like to have a pet to keep her company upstairs while her husband kept the bakery down below. This dog would be perfect, small enough not to crowd their tiny apartment, and short haired, so she wouldn't shed all over the sofa. Lilia had gathered her courage and asked Victor if they could adopt the little stray.

"Dogs are bad for business," he'd frowned. "One dog attracts more dogs — it's a bitch, you know — and customers don't want to trip over dirty strays on their way to purchase a tart."

"I'd keep her inside," Lilia had persisted more than she should have. "She'd be clean and quiet. Please let's consider this."

Now the little dog was nowhere to be seen. They'd heard rumors, Lilia and her husband, about stray dogs being captured for the government's scientific experiments, and Lilia wondered with a shudder what these experiments might entail.

"You'd best not worry yourself about it," Victor would later admonish her when she'd mention to him that the dog had disappeared. He'd never liked dogs, anyway, and one less stray on the streets was fine with him. When they'd come around the bakery asking about small mongrels, between one and six years old, females with primarily light-colored hair, he thought of the little dog his wife had mentioned, but not until they opened their wallets did he volunteer the information.

Never would he admit this to his wife. He'd done what was best for both of them, and for his business. Lilia would never have understood the complexity of this decision he'd made for them. Now they had extra money in the bank, and no stray dogs roaming the street below.

Lilia was still fretting about the little dog when her sister Galina hurried into the kitchen to pour herself a cup of the coffee Lilia had just made, so Lilia asked her sister if she knew anything about the government experimenting with stray dogs. Galina's eyebrows shot up in surprise, and Lilia knew that her sister, a photographer-trainee for the Soviet news bureau, had seen or heard something she wasn't supposed to tell.

"Please, Galina," Lilia begged her, describing the little dog in detail, "just let me know if you see her. I'm so worried."

Galina learned against the kitchen counter, thoughtfully stirring her coffee before responding.

"Why are you wearing so much makeup early in the morning?" she asked Lilia, abruptly changing the subject. A determined professional, Galina could not afford complete honesty, even with her sister. "Your cheeks are red as ripe strawberries."

"Victor likes to see me this way," Lilia replied solemnly, not mentioning the nighttime incident that had prompted her to attend to her make-up first thing this morning, blending soft circles of rouge on each cheek until both were identically rosy.

Galina was younger, not married, and nearly late for work, so she did not take time to consider her sister's complicated life. Instead she set her coffee cup down, grabbed Lilia's hand mirror, which had been resting on the kitchen table, and checked her own face, using one hand to crimp the soft curls framing her forehead. She wet her lips until they shone and pinched a subtle pink into each cheek. Her own makeup routine completed, she handed the mirror to her sister.

"Take a good look at yourself," she admonished Lilia as she rinsed her coffee cup in the sink, and gathered her camera bag and purse, preparing to leave for her job, "and make sure you please yourself as well."

A soft kiss on the cheek and Galina was gone. Lilia examined herself in the mirror, then pulled a tissue from her apron pocket to wipe away some of the rouge she'd applied earlier. The mark Victor had left was fading already. She observed herself again and was satisfied. She put the mirror away and turned up the volume on the radio to keep her company as she cleaned the kitchen. She kept glancing out the window as she worked, hoping the little stray would show up and that Victor eventually would reconsider. She pictured the little dog following her around the kitchen as she worked, jumping into her lap when she finally sat down to rest. She'd be happy petting her little dog, smoothing its fur and talking to it like an old friend, until the dog's ears perked up suddenly to catch an approaching sound.

It would be Victor, closing the bakery mid-afternoon and climbing the stairs back up to the apartment. When he opened the door, the dog was gone, and his wife, in a clean dress and fresh makeup, hurried to greet him.

7.

Overnight, my world had shrunk to the size of a bread-box, the uncomfortable cage I was supposed to call home so tiny there was barely enough room to stand up and turn around. It's hard work, when so cramped, to scratch in all the necessary places. And that long-legged, luxurious stretching routine all dogs enjoy was impossible.

Our keepers, quiet women in white shoes and smocks, brought us food, cleaned our cages, and twice a day took us outside to play, where we were still confined inside a larger enclosure from which no escape seemed possible. There was no meat in this place, nor any kind of dog food we'd ever seen, only small, soft lozenges of gray mud, but we ate them anyway because otherwise we'd starve.

At first I barked frequently and vigorously, trying to incite the others to complain with me, but most had been here so long that they remembered no other homes, and, unlike me, claimed to be satisfied with their accommodations, with established routines and with the occasional adventure some had experienced.

"What adventure?" I felt compelled to ask, if only to alleviate my boredom.

The dogs called Albina and Kozyavka told of being closed up in a box, and a fire was lit underneath. The box exploded upward, and they were pushed into the sky, higher and higher. Their souls were turned inside out. They gave up their struggles and floated briefly over the land, then returned suddenly, crashing downward, their guts churning, until a white canopy opened overhead, just in time to cushion their return to Earth. They both agreed that they'd trusted the box in which they were enclosed, the fire that sent them aloft, and the white canopy that brought them safely home. Albina, who had done this more than once, voiced her absolute faith in the human who had chosen and prepared her for these adventures.

"Afterwards he scratched my tummy and fed me treats," she explained to me. The other dogs whined in verification, but she interrupted with a sudden cry of delight. Her tail began wagging madly as the door opened and an odd-looking creature entered the room.

"That's him," Albina whispered eagerly. "That's Gazenko!"

I observed his wide forehead, prominent nose and oversized ears, seemingly hound-like, but he was definitely human. As he approached our cages, a broad grin emerged beneath his fuzzy moustache, revealing big white teeth, and instantly I recognized the human who'd captured me. It was this Gazenko who had upset my very being, taken me away from my home and locked me inside this cramped prison. I bristled and growled. He skirted my cage and moved on to greet the others, who were thrilled to see him. They pranced and yelped until their silly tongues hung wearily from their mouths.

"What good has come of all your tail-wagging?" I asked them after he'd left the room. Finally I got them to admit they'd gotten no extra privileges for their good-girl efforts.

"But why must you sulk so?" Albina countered. "It will do you no good here," and the others whined in agreement.

I told them I was angry because I was in this fix, and that I planned to stay that way. I tended to hold on to my anger, and to express it over and over, usually with a small turd, carefully placed. Now my anger demanded a more dramatic expression. I envisioned a series of containers that I'd fill, depositing some anger in each, but always retaining enough to carry forward.

"Well then, do it, but don't spend the rest of your life on it," one of them said when I'd described the extent of my rage. All dogs understand the undeniable message a well-placed turd can carry.

"You'll know you're done when you can't muster the anger to keep going with it," another one said. I had to admit there was wisdom in this dog's observation. When I could no longer poop my anger, I'd be done.

So I'd started. The other dogs complained of irregularity and blamed it on the ridiculous food they served us, but my rage easily overcame my diet. Even pooping was compromised here; the only place to do it was right in the cage, so I'd become determined to fill my cage with poop. The confusing part was that Gazenko appreciated my turds; it seemed important to him that my poop come out well — and often. Every time I'd create a new one, he'd praise me for it; one of the white-coated ladies would come in and take it away, and I'd have to start all over again. When I realized he was pleased, I tried to stop pooping, but could not; I was as regular as the sunrise. Finally I had to admit that my plan was not working. Once again this human had thwarted me; I was still seething with anger and had no way to unload my rage.

"Hello there," he'd greet me each morning as he cautiously approached my cage, wearing thick gloves to protect himself. Besides examining my stools, he listened to my heart several times a day and looked inside my mouth and ears incessantly; after every meal, he shone a tiny light down my throat. Everything he witnessed, he wrote in a small notebook he kept in one pocket of his white coat. When I curled up my mouth and let a low growl escape, he wrote this down, too. Whenever he got close, I tried to nip him, but he was surprisingly nimble and averted the danger almost effortlessly. Then he pulled out his notebook and wrote it down. I wondered out loud why this man was so obsessed with my behavior and my bodily functions.

"He's a doctor," the others explained, but this was just a word they'd heard our keepers use when referring to him. They had no idea what it meant, and I told them so.

"This is what doctors do," they insisted, another startling leap of ignorance on their part. Dogs are not the brightest creatures on this Earth; their lack of clarity and blatant misuse of logic sometimes astounds me.

"Hmph," I replied, turning away and settling down for a private sulk-fest, but I could not stop thinking about Gazenko. Most humans I can figure out instantly, but already I sensed this one was more complicated. Eventually I'd spend far too much time trying to describe him: outwardly charming yet inwardly manipulative, weak but with a strong veneer. I'd come to understand how his powerful emotions sometimes bulldozed his weaker will power. I'd learn he was demanding, uncompromising and ultimately deceitful, with only an occasional and poorly timed regret. Forty years from now, for example, the man I'd learn to love and then love to hate and then hate to love yet again, would tell the world he shouldn't have done what he would soon do to me:

"The more time passes," he would say, "the more sorry I have become. We did not learn enough from the mission to justify the death of the dog."

Such belated hindsight would be of no use at all to a long-gone dog like me.

8.
October 12, 1957

The Chief Designer had been ordered to do the impossible. He must build a new, hurry-up mission around a space dog who had not yet been chosen or trained. He must retrofit one of his massive R-7 rockets and re-engineer its fragile payload. He must ship the oversized pieces to the top-secret launch site, then hurry there himself to oversee final assembly before the whole thing was rolled to the launch pad, fueled, ignited and — if all preparations had been successful — launched into Earth orbit. He was a man of action, however, and by the next afternoon, the appropriate phone calls had been placed and he stood once again inside the Kremlin, shaking Khrushchev's outstretched hand and promising the Soviet leader that he and his workers could design and deliver Sputnik 2 — and its canine passenger — on time and on target, to maintain first place in the ever-escalating global space race.

"Yes, good," Khrushchev smiled broadly, eagerly dismissing his Chief Designer so the work could commence. The Soviet leader had done his part; he'd authorized the mission, and now he must wait patiently while everyone else scrambled to carry out his orders. Soon enough he would stand high on a platform in Red Square, waving to cheering crowds below, saluting as stiff-legged soldiers paraded past. Red flags would flap in excitement and newsreel cameras would roll, showing the world how Soviet citizens turn out to celebrate both the anniversary of the Revolution and another superb space triumph.

The Chief Designer would miss the pageantry; he would spend this celebratory day, as he spent all others, hard at work and away from the public eye. For years he and his associates had been toiling away in their miserable Design Bureau, an abandoned artillery plant just outside Moscow, with a leaky roof, no heat and no real furniture, to develop long-range missiles — now close to perfection — based on German plans they'd captured at the end of World War Two. The missile was just the launch vehicle, however; the payload was what really mattered, and that's where The Chief Designer and the Central Committee of the Communist Party, who funded his Design Bureau, had divergent opinions. While The Chief Designer envisioned a payload that would engage in scientific research, the Central Committee, pressured by the military brass, argued aggressively for launching weaponry into space.

The clever Chief Designer would have it both ways; he'd proposed development of the first Sputnik as part of a test for the long-range missile program, certain this would be approved, and it was. This success had doubled his workload, but no matter: he'd slept less and worked harder.

Last summer The Chief Designer had launched a secret missile that had traveled halfway around the world before hitting its ocean target. The payload, a fake thermonuclear bomb, proved his missile could indeed function as a potential weapon. The Central Committee was mightily pleased by this success, and now the military development of space had become The Chief Designer's designated mission. Even so, he privately maintained his personal goal of designing sophisticated technology for space exploration. Every morning, after a few hours' rest, he rose to do the military's bidding, but also busied himself, mostly in the wee hours, designing the object he planned to launch as the first Soviet satellite, to orbit the Earth and conduct scientific research in outer space.

When Khrushchev received top-secret word that the Americans were close to launching *their* satellite into space, he decided the Soviets must hurry with their plans. Suddenly The Chief Designer had a green light for his satellite, but no time to perfect his design, so he abandoned his own Sputnik plans and in just over a month, hastily assembled an alternative "Prostreishy Sputnik" (simple satellite), a shiny little sphere containing only a radio transmitter and batteries to run it. He threw in one "scientific instrument" — a thermometer — and got the whole thing off the ground and into the history books. Just for show.

The Sputnik now orbiting overhead, its radio transmitter emitting that annoying beep-beep-beep three times each second, was certainly not the scientific research satellite he'd intended to launch, nor did it house any kind of space weapon, for which the Soviet military had lobbied. Sputnik 1 had no purpose beyond being first and being noticed.

At most, The Chief Designer considered Sputnik a modest accomplishment. On the other hand, his dual successes — launching the artificial satellite into Earth orbit just weeks after launching the fake warhead — proved what he'd thought all along, that the Soviets could exercise their military might and also conduct proper scientific research in outer space. He was privately amused that the first Sputnik ended up doing neither, but quite serious about moving forward, hoping at last to finish the larger, more sophisticated satellite he'd been forced to set aside, the one that would be able to carry an additional load into space, equipped to conduct actual research. He'd been preparing for a late December launch, which he considered a reasonable deadline, when suddenly he'd been blindsided by the boss.

There was no way, even working around the clock, to have his original satellite ready to launch by November 7, the fortieth anniversary of the Bolshevik Revolution. Many of its vital parts were still on the drawing board and had yet to be fabricated; then the assembling, the testing, and the troubleshooting, which would take weeks — even without the added complication of canine life support.

By the time he shook Khrushchev's hand and left the Kremlin, however, The Chief Designer knew he would succeed because he could not afford to fail. Sputnik 2, a spacecraft he could barely visualize today, would be built and launched into Earth orbit, and it would carry the first living, breathing space passenger. All of this would be accomplished in time for a grand public celebration on November 7. In a private ceremony soon after the holiday, he surely would be awarded another Soviet medal, which he'd hide with the others inside a woolen sock he kept in the top drawer of his bedroom bureau. He'd shown them to Nina once.

"You must make sure I'm buried in these," he'd told her.

She'd nodded wisely, a loyal wife with an anonymous husband, dreading the day his name would become known to all.

9.

A confidential notice had been issued to the Soviet news outlets. The government's "rocket dogs" would be on display at the Institute of Aviation and Space Medicine, and their trainer would be available for an interview. What was even more intriguing, it was rumored that one of the dogs would soon be launched into outer space on a new secret rocket that was being built. Galina was summoned by her boss, the photography director at TASS.

"This is Khrushchev's special idea," he told her. "He wants another satellite launched right away, in time for the Bolshevik anniversary. There will be a living creature on board, a small dog. You will go there and take glorious pictures of the dogs and of their trainer."

Galina, still a news photographer in training, knew she'd just been handed a prized assignment, one that could well determine her future with the news bureau. She cleaned her gear carefully and loaded film into her Rolleiflex, then sat quietly as a taxi drove her to the Institute, trying to pre-visualize what she might be required to photograph, her special skill that she felt gave her an advantage. She imagined small dogs in a kennel. The camera angle should be low, at canine level. These photos would be all about the dogs, true Soviet heroes.

When she arrived, a brisk woman in a white lab coat met her and ushered her into the kennel area. Along the way, Galina removed the lens cap and held her camera steady, at waist-level, ready to push the shutter as she entered the large room where other reporters and photographers were gathering. While everyone was busy positioning themselves and their cameras, Galina managed quickly to set the aperture and adjust focus, then shoot six or seven pictures unnoticed. This was her other special skill, a way of taking photos surreptitiously, resulting in candid moments no other Soviet news photographer had managed to master. She even knew how to time the pressing of the shutter with someone's cough or speech, hiding the mechanical noise entirely.

A tall man with a narrow chin and a neat brown moustache stood in the middle of the room, surrounded by dogs in cages. He was introduced as Dr. Oleg Gazenko, the biomedical specialist in charge of training the dogs. The doctor looked over the small media contingent, making brief eye contact with Galina, who took this as a good sign, and edged closer. Aside from the white-coated assistant who'd greeted her at the door, she was the only woman present.

Dr. Gazenko began this press meeting with a dramatic event; he pulled two dogs from their cages and held them high above his head, one in each hand, introducing them as Albina and Kozyavka, both experienced "rocket dogs." Here at the Institute there were rocket dogs and soon there would be space dogs, he explained. Rocket dogs had already been launched in low-altitude vehicles, parachuting safely back to Earth after traveling high into the atmosphere, but just shy of outer space. Albina and Kozyavka, he pointed out, were happy and healthy, and had suffered no ill effects from their adventure.

Rather than ride a brief, parabolic curve up and down, the first space dog, not yet chosen, would go higher and farther — above the Earth's atmosphere and into Earth orbit. While in space, the dog would become entirely weightless for an extended time, and would provide critical biomedical information as eventual plans would be made to send humans into space.

Galina, watching more than she was listening, inched closer to Dr. Gazenko and the two dogs, squatted underneath and pointed her camera up for a low-angle shot. Then another. She was thinking her photographs would make people think of the dogs high above them in space, while Gazenko, who'd noticed her careful approach, imagined that in the photographs she was taking, he would look tall and heroic. Suddenly she interrupted his reverie.

"Dr. Gazenko," Galina put her camera down, stood and looked him in the eye. "I have just noticed something, that these two dogs are females. Are all your dogs female?"

Gazenko returned her gaze. "You are most observant," he replied. "Yes, we've recruited only female dogs to train for rocket and space flight."

"Surely not because you think females are stronger and braver than males," she had a curious smile as she asked.

"I can't say for sure," he matched her smile. "These dogs are all smart. They are all strong and brave. But there is another, very practical reason why we have chosen them."

He lowered the two dogs to the counter in front of him and waited expectantly for someone to ask why. Someone did.

"The canine carrier is small and the dogs who become passengers are not able to move about a great deal. As you all know, girl dogs need only squat when they urinate, while males lift one of their hind legs. We do not have room for leg lifting."

A soft titter flowed through the crowd and Gazenko watched the woman photographer to see how she reacted, but her smile never wavered.

"I see." She put the camera to her eye again and snapped a few more photos of Gazenko, then asked, "Are there any other requirements for the first space dog?"

"Yes, she must be able to sit still for a long period of time, and she must remain calm. We are training all our dogs to do this. We're also training them to eat nutritious food delivered in gelatin form."

"Anything else?" someone asked.

Gazenko thought for a moment. "She must have light colored fur."

Most all of the press representatives now had puzzled expressions; what difference could the color of a dog's coat make, one asked, but it was Galina who promptly answered.

"Contrast," she said, looking toward Gazenko for confirmation. He nodded and smiled at her again.

"That's correct. Outer space is a very dark place," he paused for effect, "but of course we will send a camera along to photograph this historic event. The white fur will show up better in the pictures."

Before the press conference ended, Galina and the other press representatives were allowed to get closer to the other dogs, the ones still in cages. Galina was careful to stoop to their level and take good, close-up shots of each and every dog; most likely one of these would become the heroic first space dog.

"Are there any more dogs being trained here?" she turned to ask Dr. Gazenko, but he'd already left the room.

"We have many dogs here," the female assistant answered her instead. "These are the dogs who have passed preliminary tests only."

"Then when will the space dog be chosen? Will we be invited back to see her?" Galina persisted, but the assistant offered no more answers. Instead, one by one, she began carrying the dogs in their cages into another room, concentrating exclusively on her task. The press conference had come to a sudden conclusion.

Information may flow freely from government agencies to the government's news media, but as Galina had just observed, there are strict controls over what and how much can be revealed, and some inquiries signal an abrupt halt to the flow. What the young photographer did not know was that asking too many questions might also trigger the government's interest in watching the questioner for any future sign of suspicious behavior — which the government might well decide to call "subversive activity."

10.

Lilia had made the beds, mopped the kitchen floor and scrubbed the sink and countertop clean; now she sat resting in her sunny upstairs window, watching sparse morning activity in the street below. The barrister had already been by for his muffins and then had retreated to his quiet office next door, when she saw the door to the rectory open. The young priest stepped outside in his cleric's robe, wearing thin bedroom slippers, a woolen scarf wrapped around his neck and shoulders. He stood shivering in the morning chill, not moving from his doorstep, but looking intently up and down the street. There was nothing to see.

He went back inside, shutting the door, but emerged again a few minutes later, now wearing boots, a long overcoat and a wide-brimmed black hat trimmed with silver studs, which made him look, improbably, like a winter cowboy going out for a ride on the range. Instead, he walked slowly, methodically, down one side of the street and back up the other, stopping at each doorway, alleyway or the smallest crevice between structures. Once Lilia thought she heard him whistle softly.

When he arrived at the front door of the bakery, he paused for a moment, taking in the delicious smells of the cakes and tarts he so seldom had money to buy, then entered, jingling the little bells on the shop door.

Lilia could no longer sit still. She left the window and crept down the back stairs, secreting herself just behind the thin wooden door that separated the stairs from the bakery itself.

"Good morning, Father," she heard her husband greet the priest, slight surprise creeping into his voice. "You've come to choose a morning treat for yourself?"

The priest removed his big hat, thinking about what answer he should offer.

"That smallest fruit tart," he pointed to the products underneath a glass dome on the counter. "How much would it cost?" He fumbled inside his overcoat, pretending to search for change.

"Please, Father, take one." Victor lifted the glass dome and allowed the priest to choose his treat. "No charge to you."

The priest selected the smallest tart and wrapped it in the sheet of wax paper Victor handed him. He thanked the baker, but did not leave the shop.

The baker wondered briefly whether the priest had another motive for stopping by — perhaps to discuss his eternal life? Victor, a good communist, eschewed religion, and his Lilia, though less strident about all things spiritual, had not attended mass since they were married. Victor began wondering whether he, an atheist, could pray now for the arrival of another customer, so as to cut short the priest's visit.

"I'm wondering," the priest ventured, pocketing his tart, "whether you've noticed a little stray dog in the neighborhood? Short-haired, a mixed breed, mostly white, with some brown markings on the face." The priest used his hands to mime the dog's size and markings.

Behind the door, Lilia drew in her breath.

"Oh, yes, I remember that mutt," Victor replied cautiously. "But lately I've not seen her. Maybe she's been taken in by some kind neighbor."

"I've asked everyone I know, and I've put a notice up in the church vestibule."

"Oh, well, then surely someone will find her." The baker became busy arranging his products, though they were perfectly arranged before. "Or else she'll show up again, when she's good and hungry. That's the way it is with strays, you know."

The priest realized he would get no information here; there was no point in lingering.

"You'll let me know if you see the dog?" he asked the baker. Victor said of course he would.

The priest left the bakery, closing the door tightly behind him, jingling its bells again, and strolled briskly back toward the rectory, where a woman wearing a frilly apron instead of an overcoat was sitting on his doorstep, hugging herself tightly with her own bare arms to retain body warmth.

"I am sorry, Father, that I have sinned," she began, but he interrupted her gently.

"If you are coming to confess, you should wait until noon. That's when confession time starts."

The woman continued as if she had not heard him.

"I've just eavesdropped on my husband. I should not have done that."

"And you're so regretful about that, you've come out in the bitter cold to confess to it?" The priest marveled at this woman's sanctity. If she considered this a serious offense, she must truly be a good soul, and he had to admit he did not encounter many good souls these days. He yearned to know this soul better, but inside, where it was warmer.

"I'm about to make myself a strong pot of tea," he said. "Would you like to come inside, have some tea and warm yourself up?"

Minutes later, Lilia, wrapped in a thin blanket the priest had provided, sipped a steaming cup of tea, and told the priest about the conversation she'd overheard between him and her husband.

"I know this dog you're looking for; I'm worried, too."

She told him of the noises she'd heard in the street one night, and that the little dog had not been seen since.

"But of course your husband may be right. The dog may have wandered off to another neighborhood and someone kind may have taken him in."

"Her — she's a girl dog."

"Sometimes it's hard to tell with strays."

"She'd squat and pee outside the barrister's office, every morning, like clockwork."

Lilia realized she'd embarrassed them both; she lowered her face, hiding behind the steam rising from her teacup. When she looked up again, an odd picture nailed crookedly to one wall caught her eye: a black-clad cowboy. On another wall she located a more familiar white-robed and halo-ed Jesus. Both men were handsome and both smiled at her; automatically she smiled back. Her gaze traveled to the priest, sitting in his rocking chair, midway between the cowboy and the Christ, and her smile continued.

The priest smiled back uncomfortably; he'd felt something oddly remote for one in his profession. He'd been charmed by this woman, and he wanted desperately to be charmed by her again.

11.

The others liked to gossip about Gazenko; they were amused at how he'd transformed himself in front of the company that had recently come calling. Normally a solemn man who seldom spoke more than one sentence at a time, when placed in front of an audience, Gazenko had become talkative and almost giddy.

"He went on and on about how brilliant, how obedient and how even-tempered we all are," one had bragged.

That explains why I wasn't invited, I thought to myself. Gazenko knew he could not count on me for good behavior in front of visitors.

"And he introduced each of us by name," another added with pride.

I knew about the silly names: Albina ("Whitey"), Kozyavka ("Little Gnat"), Snezhinka ("Snowflake"), and Otvazhnaya ("Brave One"). Whenever our keepers thought of a new one, they'd write it on a card and attach it to one of our cages. I checked my cage each morning; so far no one had named me, and the anonymity suited me just fine.

"Humans like to name things," I told them. "That's how they tell us apart, which proves they're idiots; we're all so different one from another."

At least I'm different from all of you with silly names stuck to your cages, I thought silently to myself with some dignity.

Visitors were a rare event, but before long another showed up, and this one was allowed to see us all. Today's guest, a man wearing a dark suit and broad-brimmed hat tilted so that his face was nearly hidden, appeared with a small contingent of other well-dressed humans; they were escorted through with great deference. The one in front, tall and broad-shouldered — mastiff-like — seemed important; when he paused, everyone paused, and when he walked, they all walked in step behind him — even the great Gazenko, who did not jabber on and on as the others had predicted, but spoke only when spoken to.

The visitor was not willing to dawdle, but stopped long enough to lean down and look carefully at each one of us crouched in our cage. That's when I noticed his sad eyes, his wide forehead wrinkled with worry, and the constant frown that occupied his face. I didn't know at the time he was The Chief Designer, the one who would send me to my death in one of his fire-breathing missiles. I didn't know that he'd come here to instruct Gazenko on the details of the upcoming launch; already the clock was ticking.

"Then how will you choose?" I heard this visitor ask.

"I have a method," Gazenko explained. "Every day the cages are adjusted, and the space they occupy becomes more limited."

He used his hands to demonstrate how much, then continued, "Some whine and wiggle to be set free. These will not be successful. Eventually one will prevail and she's the one I will choose."

He paused in front of my cramped cage as he said this. I glared at him mutely.

"This new one," he gestured toward me, "she has a ways to go, but she's making good progress, and we still have some time."

Suddenly he thrust his index finger through the metal bars of my cage. I resisted the urge to spring forward and snap it off; instead I huddled in the back corner, and this time I kept quiet, calm and still. Gazenko, for the first time ever, smiled at me before moving away, the bristly corners of his big fuzzy moustache curving upward, lips parted to reveal his perfect teeth.

"Good dog," he whispered in the same low, emotionless voice he'd used when he'd captured me, as if trying to conceal his actual feelings, but I could tell he was pleased with me.

What was disquieting about this? Not that I'd learned how to make this despicable man smile, but that part of me wanted to do this again.

Never, ever let down your guard around a human just because he treats you nicely.

I wish now that I'd listened more carefully to my own advice.

12.

"So much is being asked of you, and so little time remains, but I'm confident that together we will persevere. We will do whatever the mission requires of us. We must not fail."

The uncomfortable building that housed the Soviet Design Bureau was alive again, and The Chief Designer toiled alongside his staff to construct the new satellite and launch vehicle. He spent a little time each day trying, in his own solemn way, to build the workers' morale, not by praising their efforts, but by reminding them how much responsibility rested on their shoulders, and that, in spite of the fast approaching deadline, they could not afford to cut corners.

"We will not have time to create special drawings, or to make repeated quality checks, but still our work must be perfect. I ask each of you to let your own conscience guide you through the process, as my own conscience will guide me."

He moved his gaze around the group of assembled workers, pausing to look each one directly in the eye as he said this. Then with a wave of his hand, he sent them all back to their jobs and returned to his.

I don't know exactly when this man first realized that in order for Sputnik 2 to be a success and for the leader Khrushchev to be pleased, the space dog had to die. Surely he was aware of the parachutes that had returned Albina and Kozyavka safely to Earth. Surely there was a way to pack a small parachute into the spaceship, and to make it operational before the passenger perished either in the cold vacuum of space or during a fiery re-entry.

Surely, because I like to believe the best about this sad-eyed man, he spent some agonizing hours at his design bench, perhaps just after he'd seen us at the kennel, slide rule at the ready, pencil in hand, hopeful for some inspiration that would help him solve this life-or-death dilemma. As usual, he worked far into the night; his associates marveled at how little sleep he was getting and how well he continued to function.

"Production is a continuous process," he'd reminded them, "and one that is best not interrupted."

He did not believe in wasting time on sleep, when time was growing more precious each day and when he had so much to accomplish during his waking hours. Except for today's brief visit to observe the dogs and meet with their trainer, he had not left the warehouse for days, choosing to nap instead on the cot he'd set up in a closet. He was not surprised when the dream he could never escape found him dozing there:

Just after midnight and the police come pounding on his door; he awakes with a start. He's told nothing as he's taken from his home and family without even a change of clothes, although his wife manages to slip a pair of clean undershorts into his pocket as they drag him away from her.

He's had this dream so many times he already knows where he's headed, to Kolyma, in far-away Siberia, sentenced to ten years in a place where most prisoners die within the first year, of starvation, cold or mistreatment.

From sunup to sunset he was forced to dig for gold in the frozen earth and was rarely fed enough to fuel his efforts. If he stopped digging, he was beaten soundly. It was his great fortune that another imprisoned rocket scientist, Andrei Tupolev, discovered his whereabouts and requested his transfer to a *sharaga*, a specialized prison unit just outside Moscow, where the weather was better, the feedings more regular, and the treatment much less severe. There he, Tupolev and others still spent their long days in forced labor for the Soviet government, but now they were doing the rocketry R&D they enjoyed. Even so, the door was locked from the outside and leaving to go home at the end of a workday was out of the question.

Although he'd been released from the *sharaga* when the war ended, his official status as a political prisoner had not changed until just a few months ago, when he was "rehabilitated," a long overdue pardon which finally liberated him from his "criminal" past.

Korolev awoke suddenly on his cot in the Design Bureau, then lay there for a while wrestling with his conscience, telling himself he could not afford to waste valuable time over concerns about the dog's survival. He'd passed the mid-point; the launch window was now just over two weeks away, and he knew there would be no reprieve for the small passenger aboard Sputnik 2. As he and Dr. Gazenko had agreed during their meeting earlier today, the dog would travel in a modified version of the canine carrier used on earlier rocket flights, but because this trip would be longer, they'd add an automated feeder to deliver meals on a regular schedule. The dog would be fully "bioinstrumented" (a word Gazenko had used), and all life signs telemetered back to Earth. This time, in addition to Sputnik's mechanical beep, earthlings would hear something far more dramatic: the passenger's heartbeat.

Above the dog's travel compartment would sit the familiar round duplicate of Sputnik 1, this time housing more sophisticated communications equipment and batteries to power it all.

On the outside this Sputnik would have the same cone-shaped shroud as Sputnik 1 to protect its contents during the explosive launch; the cover would be jettisoned from the spacecraft once it reached orbit, but this time the spacecraft would remain attached to the third stage of the missile. It was a shortcut that made sense, using the third stage of the rocket itself as part of the satellite. This way the rocket and payload could share the same telemetry system, he could use the rocket's guidance system to stabilize the spacecraft, and he could avoid the weight of an onboard separation device.

Because this Sputnik would be bigger, it would be easier to spot as it crossed the night sky, and its improved telemetry system would transmit back to tracking centers on Earth an incredible amount of information about the trip into space, the condition of the satellite inside and out, and the progress of its passenger. After a week to ten days, the batteries would run down, the telemetry and life-support functions would cease, and the dog would die.

Gazenko had insisted he see the dogs during his visit to the Institute today; the doctor was proud of his dogs and wanted to demonstrate how well they were being trained.

Once inside the kennel, The Chief Designer had leaned down to look each dog in the eye, his way of establishing a respectful rapport with those with whom he shared this mission. Now the dogs were visible in his mind; he could not so easily dismiss the unsuspecting one who would become Sputnik's doomed passenger. After his own gulag experience, he'd vowed never to treat another living creature as anything less, a promise that was becoming increasingly hard to keep.

Not all of the earlier rocket dogs had survived their trips, he reminded himself. Some had crashed to their deaths when their parachutes failed; others had died when their rockets exploded in flight, but these were accidents, not deliberate acts — *though they might well have been.* The Chief Designer was the only person who knew about the secret explosive device included in all rocket dog flights; he was the one who'd push the button to blow up any rocket veering off target, about to land in enemy territory. He'd never had to push the button; he'd never before had to intentionally kill a dog.

Now in its runaway rush to glory, the Soviet government had imposed its stiffest penalty on the first space dog, and The Chief Designer had been named executioner. Instead of trying to save the dog, he wondered whether poison, delivered automatically in the last meal, would be more humane.

13.

That evening after Victor had gone to bed, Galina spread her photos across the kitchen table for her sister to examine: close-ups of two beautiful dogs, one with fluffy white fur, sparkling eyes, and a pointed snout topped by a tiny moist nose; the other smaller with shorter hair, mostly white with scattered dark markings. More dogs in cages, nudging their noses toward the camera, eyes wide and ears perked as Galina had clicked away. Lilia held each photo up to the light and examined it carefully.

"No," Lilia pronounced slowly and sadly. "I don't see the little dog I knew."

"I'm sorry." Galina quickly gathered the photos back into the brown envelope and hid the envelope deep inside her purse. "I thought she might be one of these."

It was past midnight; Victor's snoring rumbled from the next room.

"You cannot tell anyone I showed these to you," she admonished her sister. "Not even Victor."

"I will not tell a soul," Lilia promised, full of gratitude for her younger sister's unanticipated generosity. Earlier today, while in the darkroom printing the photographs, Galina had taken time to consider her sister's simple request, and had printed an extra set, which she'd hidden in the bottom of her purse before coming home. No one would know this.

"Do you have sugar?" Galina asked, and Lilia, who took her coffee black, got up and searched through her cabinets. Victor always had sugar for his baking; there was usually a small tin for the household.

The sisters were enjoying razor-thin slices of leftover pound cake from the bakery and Lilia had reheated the morning coffee, producing a tiny carton of real cream from her small refrigerator to mediate the stale taste.

"Will you go there again?" Lilia asked as her sister sweetened, stirred and tasted her coffee, then deemed it drinkable.

"Maybe so. There was a man working there who seemed to notice me."

Lilia pulled her chair closer to the table.

"You must tell me about him," she coaxed her sister. "Was he tall? And was he good-looking?"

"Yes, I think he was. He had brown eyes, brown hair... nice straight teeth...and a bristly moustache." A rare giggle escaped Galina. She pulled another photo from her purse. "Here, decide for yourself."

Lilia studied the picture of a man holding two dogs high in the air. He was smiling and looking directly into the camera.

"I'd call him handsome," Lilia decided quickly. "What's his name?"

"Dr. Oleg Gazenko. He's in charge of training the dogs there."

What good fortune, Lilia thought, but did not say. My sister has a new boyfriend who knows the dogs. We will be able to find out whether my little dog is there.

"Please don't ask me more," Galina spoke again, as if reading her sister's mind. She put the picture of Gazenko and the dogs back in her purse. "I will find out what I can, when I can, but I can't take too many risks with my job. You know that."

"Can you at least flirt with him?" Lilia knew how stubbornly Galina elevated her budding career above all else, even romance.

"Flirting with Oleg," Galina smiled dreamily, "will not be a problem."

14.

Galina did not have to wait very long to see Dr. Gazenko again. The next day, she was summoned by her boss. Another set of the photographs she'd shown her sister last evening were spread on the desk before him: pretty white Albina, charmingly rumpled Kozyavka, the tall and dignified Dr. Gazenko, the other caged dogs. Galina's boss looked up as she entered the room and wordlessly motioned for her to sit down. She sat and waited for him to speak, but when he did not, she decided to begin the conversation herself.

"You asked to see me, sir," she ventured. "Are my photos acceptable to you?"

"Why do you ask such questions?" He shook his head, irritated. "Why did you ask such questions at yesterday's press conference? Don't you know you are not a reporter? You are a photographer."

"Yes, sir," she answered, her usual confidence rapidly shrinking.

Her boss held up the photograph of Oleg Gazenko with the two dogs and shook it in front of her face. "This is an important man, and you bombard him with drivel!" He continued in a silly, falsetto voice. "Are girls smarter than boys? And braver? Is that why girls will be first to go into space?"

Galina, amazed to hear her own words tossed back at her, kept quiet and looked down at her hands folded in her lap. She wondered exactly how much trouble she was in, and whether she was about to be fired.

"Reporters ask questions. Photographers take pictures. Remember that," her boss snarled.

"Yes, sir, of course. I'm very sorry to have overstepped my bounds. This will not happen again."

After another long pause, she ventured to look up and was surprised to see a wry smile creeping across his lips.

"Good." He seemed satisfied by her apology. "Now I will answer the question you have asked me."

"You don't have to do that, sir," she hurried to say, now absolutely humbled. "It was incorrect of me to ask what you think of my photographs. Of course you will comment on my work as you deem appropriate."

Her boss continued as if he had not heard her. "You have done very well," he told her. "And, by the way, this very important doctor who trains the space dogs telephoned me this morning. He has asked to see your photographs. I believe you have made a good impression. Will you please make another set of prints and deliver them to him?"

"I will be most happy to do that." Galina rose from her seat, about to excuse herself, then sat back down abruptly. She looked at her boss and he looked at her, grinning but saying nothing. She fidgeted in her chair until she could stand the silence no longer.

"Will that be all, sir?" she inquired in a tiny voice.

Her boss laughed heartily, excusing her with a wave of his hand. Galina hurried to the darkroom, mind reeling and heart pounding. She'd already done the work, the second set of photos already in her purse, awaiting delivery. The handsome and important doctor had asked to see her again — or was it only her photographs he was interested in examining?

Always confused about men and their motives, Galina promised herself she'd seek her older sister's advice this evening.

15.

My cage was shrinking; Gazenko had admitted as much to our recent visitor. My hind legs ached from having to scrunch up to sleep. I would've given anything to enjoy a full body stretch, but why stop there? I'd like to go out and look for a real meal and then I'd like to choose my own place to poop; maybe I'd even roll in it afterwards. When it was time for a nap, I'd turn myself around and around, choosing the exact time and place to settle down. What I wanted was control and I had none. I was too hot; I was too cold; but mostly, I was still mired in anger and confusion about what was happening to me.

Even worse, when I woke up this morning, I found that I had been given one of those silly names. The hand-printed sign on my cage now said "Kudryavka" — "Little Curly." I believe I'm already on record in stating how inappropriate this name was for a short-haired dog like me, and I complained irritably to the others.

"It's your ears," one of the dogs tried to explain to me. "They curl forward, you know."

"They do not." With some effort, I was able to make both my ears stand up tall and straight.

"It's your tail," another dog told me. I jerked around to see if this was true, bumping my nose of the bars of my cage as I did so. It was; even when I tried to straighten it out, my tail remained stubbornly curled up over my rear end.

"Well, one thing's for sure," another remarked to the others, plenty loud for me to overhear, "it's certainly not her nose — look at that long snout!"

No one had assessed my appearance in such critical detail as these silly girl dogs, but then they had so few ways to amuse themselves. Occasionally I felt myself falling into their trap of incessant scrutiny and superficial commentary. "Albina," for instance, was the perfect name for the dog with fluffy white fur living in the cage next door. She was pretty, and popular with both dogs and humans. Among all the dogs here, Albina was by far the friendliest, one of the oldest and the most experienced. I think the others looked toward her for leadership, and even I found her sunny disposition welcome in this otherwise horrible place. Except for the fact that she adored Gazenko, I might have considered becoming best friends with her. When he showed up this morning, she jumped up as usual, pawing the front of her cage in his direction, whining and wagging her tail in what I considered an embarrassing show of affection.

"Hello, Albina." He reached into the cage to scratch her behind the ears; she thanked him with a simpering little whine, while I nearly retched with disgust.

The other dogs followed her lead, all except me. As always, I waited anxiously to see what he had in mind for me today, and then to take time to ponder how well I'd cooperate, if at all. So far I'd learned to *sit, stay,* and *come* on voice command; there were treats involved for such compliance. I'd eaten the terrible food they provided and pooped it back out at them. Sometimes I'd sat in a tiny cage, all alone in a dark room, for a long, long time, without complaining. I'd been through much worse on the streets, and had survived; once I'd got myself stuck in a rain barrel while trying to get a drink of water, and it took me the better part of a day and night to extricate myself. Those, I thought with a sudden pang of nostalgia, were good days.

Gazenko approached my cage, sporting a smiley good mood. "And how are you, Kudryavka?"

I wanted to let him know that I was not impressed by my new name, nor by his good behavior; but I sensed he had some ulterior motive for today's pleasantries, so I decided to sit quietly until I found out more.

"That's a good girl." With bare hands he reached into my cage, but I did not attack, and this seemed to please him greatly. He looked into my mouth and ears, then scratched my back for a good, long time. That part wasn't so bad.

"You're a lucky one," Albina whispered as soon as Gazenko had checked us all and left. "He's beginning to like you."

I was so homesick. I'd been thinking all morning about my little street and the kind priest who'd been my friend, but mostly I was missing the unparalleled freedom I'd had to come and go as I pleased.

So I turned up my nose and snarled back at her, "I'd be lucky indeed if I'd never run into the human named Gazenko."

It was true what Albina and the others said, though; in the past few days Gazenko had been most generous with his praise and had begun paying special attention to me, but I was far from knowing how best to respond.

"You might just try being nice to him," Albina insisted.

"And you might just try leaving me alone." I turned my back to her before she could dispense any more of her good-girl advice.

16.

It was nearly dawn. The Chief Designer took in a rare breath of fresh cold air as he stepped outside the Design Bureau. He knew precisely when to look up and he did; there was a tiny but brilliant point of light creeping across the sky — not the first Sputnik, as most observers identified it, but its larger third stage, which, after separation, had followed its smaller payload into orbit. Sputnik could not be seen with the naked eye. He'd known since his first sketches of Sputnik that the orb would be tiny, only 58 centimeters in diameter, but it would be polished for optimal reflection in space — not only to make it more visible to ground telescopes which would track its journey, but also to reflect the sunlight, which would keep the sensitive equipment inside from overheating.

One morning, while preparing the first Sputnik, he'd emerged from a few hours of sleep in his closet, approached the satellite, noticed it had not been polished as he'd instructed, and began a loud harangue, directed at the assistant engineer on duty. His staff wondered briefly about his sanity, but decided instead to blame it on the stress and his lack of sleep. Finally another worker approached and reminded him that this was the backup model, not the one designed for launch into space.

"But this one will be displayed in museums and seen by millions," he'd justified his verbal attack. "It must be perfect as well."

The Chief Designer was known for such emotional outbursts, always followed, a few moments later, by reasonable and forgivable calmness.

Later that day, to demonstrate he meant business, he'd placed the backup, now suitably polished by the assistant who'd been disciplined, on a pedestal covered in red velvet, and invited the filmmaker he'd hired to document the building and launching of Sputnik to come with his 16mm movie camera and shoot some footage — for the archives, he'd barked to anyone who dared question his reasoning.

"It's important to make records as well as history," he'd explained.

His own history had taught him how easily one could disappear. He'd vanished twice so far, once when he was spirited off to prison, and secondly, when he'd been appointed as The Chief Designer, a post of incredible importance and absolute anonymity.

"How can you love the Soviet Union so?" a close associate had once asked him. "This is the country that sent you to die in the gulag for no good reason."

"But I did not stay there long," he'd shrugged and answered. "Now I am here, and proud to be a Soviet citizen."

"But you toil your life away in anonymity," the associate had persisted. "Surely you must question the reason why you perform such incredible feats and yet no one knows your name. No one sees your face. It's as if you are invisible."

"We cannot take chances with my security," he'd mimicked the answer the Soviet leadership had given him. "My anonymity is the reason we are so far ahead of the Americans in this so-called 'space race.'"

Now as he watched the third-stage evidence of his first satellite disappear beneath the western horizon, on its way to visit China, then America, then the Soviet Union once again, he lamented for a moment that Sputnik 2 would never achieve its original goal; it would never be displayed in historical museums. Instead, it would suffer the same fate as this Sputnik soon would, a gradual deterioration of orbit until eventually it would once again touch the Earth's atmosphere, becoming shinier and hotter than could be imagined, finally burning up and disintegrating into nothing at all.

"We will all vanish without a trace," he whispered to himself with a grimace.

He'd said this often while in the *sharaga*, where many imprisoned scientists like himself had toiled night and day in miserable studios because they had no choice. Just like now, Nina told him recently, when he'd finally had a chance to go home to her, bathe, make efficient love, change clothes and head back to work.

"You might just as well still be a prisoner," she'd lamented, and he could not disagree. She'd packed him a carton of food she'd prepared; he knew she worried about him constantly.

In those earlier days, when he'd been arrested and imprisoned, his wife had not been Nina, but Xenia. Later, under pressure, Xenia had denounced him, while he was still in the Siberian prison camp. He'd divorced Xenia as soon as he left prison; he and his first wife had not communicated since he was taken away and he knew there was no point in continuing their marriage. His daughter had stayed with Xenia, and to this day neither she nor her mother knew of his important position in the Soviet space program.

The kind and brilliant Nina had stepped in then, first as an interpreter when he and others were sent to post-war Germany to examine the remnants of Hitler's well-developed rocket industries, and then as his beloved though often ignored second wife. He wondered if some day she'd also denounce his activities as Xenia had, in order to reclaim her own freedom. The Chief Designer was well aware that his position did not allow him to be a very good husband; he could not afford the time, the energy or what he presumed to be the required emotional investment. Those who knew him best described his personality as kind yet aloof, one full of technical zeal, but lacking in human warmth.

He shivered in the cold night air and went back inside the warehouse, now eerily quiet and nearly empty. His new satellite design had been built and the necessary modifications to the R-7 rocket had been completed. Everything was still in pieces, the quickly fabricated parts loaded carefully aboard railroad cars and shipped to the secret launch site, a five-day journey, along with the workers who would be needed for the final assembly and testing. Soon he would fly to the Baikonur Cosmodrome, far away in the Kazahkstan region, to supervise completion of the new satellite and launch vehicle. He had a small house there where he could be comfortable. Always in secret, he was acknowledged as the leader. He was valued as an uncompromising but fair boss. His knowledge of rocketry was unsurpassed, even by his well-known American counterpart Werner von Braun.

"Von Braun and I should have been friends," he'd once remarked to Nina. While still in the *sharaga*, he'd taught himself some German and English, in hopeful anticipation that he'd someday join the rapidly evolving international community of rocket scientists and engineers. Such participation, he'd come gradually to realize, would be impossible for a man who did not officially exist.

Part Two

Training

1.
Baikonur Cosmodrome
October 18, 1957

The Chief Designer landed here before I did, his long flight from Moscow — like mine would be, less than two weeks later — in an oversized turbo-prop plane that could barely put itself down on the tiny airstrip laid out on the barren steppes. As seen from the air, the Baikonur Cosmodrome, named for a city located some 400 kilometers away (the deliberate mismatch between name and location for security reasons), revealed great expanses of scrubby nothingness in all directions, then a sudden cluster of plain buildings near a crossroad. A single railroad track advanced from one direction, unraveling into multiple spurs that converged near the buildings and abruptly stopped at the base of the site's most unusual structure, a square platform with complex metalwork built up from it, the whole thing resting above an enormous black hole in the ground.

This was the launch pad at the super-secret Soviet space base; two weeks ago The Chief Designer had watched in tense excitement as his workers ignited a towering R-7 rocket with tiny Sputnik 1 perched on top, the fiery exhaust scorching every centimeter of the pit underneath as the massive vehicle strained to rise from the platform. At the same time, four matching sets of metalwork that had held the rocket vertically while being prepared for launch were released, falling gracefully down and away as the R-7 and its historic payload rose slowly and steadily into the sky.

The final countdown and launch had been a gut-wrenching but ultimately gratifying moment for the Chief Designer, who had succeeded in the near-impossible dream few had tackled and none had realized: he'd designed and built a spaceship that had left Earth's atmosphere and was still circling the planet every hour and a half, beeping its position and progress through space.

"Today we've seen the realization of a dream," he offered formal remarks to his assembled workers afterwards, pausing with them briefly to savor this amazing success.

"The conquering of space has begun," he continued, with such uncharacteristic emotion that his voice broke and tears gathered in his dark eyes. "The door to the stars has opened."

He'd had no idea then that he'd be returning so soon to the launch site, preparing to accomplish yet another near-impossible task — launching the first living creature into space. He certainly had not envisioned then that the first space passenger on board his next Sputnik would be a stray mutt snatched from the Moscow streets. He hoped, as much for posterity's sake as for his own, that Gazenko would manage to train one of the prettier dogs, one that would please the public; undoubtedly her picture would appear in newspapers and magazines all over the world. She must not bring disgrace to the Soviet Union, nor to his rapidly evolving space program.

Now as The Chief Designer's airplane descended toward the launch site, he observed from his tiny window a bevy of identically clad workers cleaning and preparing the blackened pit and platform for the next adventure. He could not identify their drab uniforms from such a distance, but knew they were political prisoners brought here initially to do hurry-up manual labor — excavating bunkers, pouring concrete and erecting buildings — and kept here now to perform undesirable tasks like the one he'd just observed. Political prisoners, he thought, should not be sentenced to such horrible working conditions for "crimes" they most likely had not committed; he knew from his own gulag experience that their treatment was harsh and that some would probably die from this. On the other hand, The Chief Designer understood that without their forced contributions, his dream of space could not be realized; there was simply not enough post-war Soviet manpower to get the necessary work accomplished in so short a time. Once on the ground, he'd try his best to avoid them; if he did not have to look them in the eye, perhaps he could prevent himself from thinking of them. Saddened by such necessities, he turned away from the window and slumped into his seat until the aircraft touched down and slowly rolled to a stop.

As soon as the big propellers stopped turning and the airplane hatch was swung open, The Chief Designer hurried toward the "space room," where tall doors slid apart to reveal the shiny Sputnik, its shell still split into two halves, each perched atop a specially designed eye-level work platform, attended by men in white smocks and caps. A quick visual survey indicated that the satellite had survived its long journey by rail from Moscow. In other areas of the vast assembly building, he observed sections of the R-7 rocket and its four massive boosters still mounted on the flatbed rail cars aboard which they'd traveled here, a giant puzzle waiting for the mastermind to fit its pieces together. The Chief Designer breathed a sigh of relief that they were all in one place, the man and his creations, once again poised to make history.

Word had quickly spread among the thousands working here at the launch site that The Chief Designer was on his way; many had run outside when they heard the big plane approaching to watch it land; they all knew this man, known here as Number 20, was aboard. Some workers hurried behind him into the assembly building and approached him like an old friend, asking after his wife, offering food, suggesting he take a rest in his little cottage here, to get over the long trip, but he waved their words away. Back to business was his only interest. Of course, the workers murmured, this is his way, and they silently fell in step behind him.

Moscow, the Kremlin, his wife Nina, his comfortable home in the city, even the miserable Design Bureau where he'd lived and worked so diligently, all were forgotten now, his focus set on this time, this place, and the precious few days he had to pull it all together. There was no way to know for certain whether all elements would work as planned; there had been no testing. There would be new parts and instruments aboard, including the more robust Tral-D telemetry system, adding significant weight to the payload. Over 500 kilograms, this Sputnik was six times larger and heavier than the first, and would demand every bit of thrust his launch missile — another sturdy and powerful R-7 rocket — could muster.

Finally, in a separate room of the assembly building kept antiseptically clean and germ-free, he observed the canine passenger's space accommodations: an oval cabin with air conditioning, a luxuriously padded seat and clear round porthole that would soon provide a spectacular view of the heavens. Like the R-7 rocket parts, pieces of the cabin sat waiting for final assembly and testing, including connections to instruments inside the round Sputnik that would insure delivery of fresh oxygen and food for seven to ten days.

Although Dr. Gazenko was in charge of the space dog's training at a separate facility — the Institute of Aviation and Space Medicine — the dog's behavior here and in space would be The Chief Designer's responsibility. In his disciplined mind, the dog stood out among all other components of the missile and payload as the least predictable part of the mission; there could be barking, snarling, growling, howling, snapping, even the nipping of human flesh. He'd known dogs like this back in the gulag; he'd been bitten once by an angry guard dog with whom he'd made brief but unfortunate eye contact; he'd not been able to warm up to any dog since then.

In the back of his head, as he put on his white lab coat and reviewed a thick stack of his own handwritten notes, in preparation for supervising every task from now until the launch, The Chief Designer was acutely aware that even the very best canine training can be transitory, and a dog with serious business to conduct cannot be easily ignored.

2.
Moscow

Meanwhile back at the kennel, I was minding my own business. I'd never heard of the faraway Cosmodrome and would not have paid attention if anyone had tried to tell me about it. Such remote and fanciful information was of no use to me, stuck here with no way of seeing beyond the confines of this cage, this kennel, or this, another miserable day of imprisonment. Any prisoner will tell you that the worst part about being held captive is not knowing the duration; without this knowledge, one can only imagine the worst, that it will go on forever, every new day bringing more of the same, and each day almost too much to bear.

The others amused themselves constantly with mind-numbing gossip about themselves and about others who'd lived here before my arrival. In fact, the kennel was ripe with rumors about other dogs that had disappeared. Some had been taken away and had never returned. A few had run away from fear of what might happen to them. Although I still pretended to ignore their chatter, my ears would perk up whenever I'd overhear anything that might help me find a way out of here.

"How did the others escape?" I'd ask, but they claimed ignorance about the details. The yard where we went to exercise was enclosed on all four sides. Whenever we were not locked in our cages, we were always harnessed, attached to a leash, and so intently observed that escape seemed out of the question.

But there was the legend of Smelaya — the Bold One.

Once upon a time, the other dogs told me, she'd been a rocket dog; high-strung and terrified by the training and not knowing what would come next, she'd found a way out of the exercise yard. Some thought she'd scraped a hole, a little farther each time she was taken outside, until one day she'd pushed herself under the fence and wiggled through a narrow passageway that eventually led her to freedom.

"Good for Smelaya," I'd praised the runaway dog. Then they told me the rest of the story.

She'd come back for Gazenko. He'd taken control of her mind, they explained, and of her instincts, so that she couldn't bear to disappoint him. She knew that he needed her and that his success depended on her contribution, no matter how scary it may be for her. He'd found her crouched and shivering at the kennel door when he came to work the next morning, scooped her into his arms, told her how much he loved her, how much he'd missed her, and fed her special treats. As the story goes (most likely with some embellishment from the dogs, who had not seen any of this with their own beady little eyes or smelled it with their own moist little noses), Gazenko wept the next day when he shut her in a box atop a rocket, lit a fire under it and sent her on a treacherous journey from which he knew she might not return.

"I suppose this story is going to have a happy ending," I'd interrupted, feigning boredom. I'd heard the story about the rocket ride before, from Albina and Kozyavka, who had survived similar ordeals and were safely returned to the kennel. "Where is Smelaya now?"

There was a whispered consultation among the dogs, as if they were trying to get their story consistent.

"He took her home with him. She became his special pet."

"And they lived happily ever after, I suppose," I'd growled, quite unintentionally.

"Smelaya lives with Gazenko to this day," the other dogs insisted.

"Prove it," I'd demanded, now in quite a foul mood without knowing why.

They couldn't, of course. They said they'd overheard the man and his assistants speaking of his pet dog from time to time, but I easily dismissed this as hearsay. At the same time, I wondered feverishly if there was truth to this legend, and whether a kennel dog could become a special pet. I retreated into a sullen pout and refused to talk to them any more that day. I pushed my rear end as far back into one corner of my cage as was possible (which was not far at all), folded my front legs to cradle my chin, closed my eyes to escape them all, and eventually relaxed into my mid-morning nap.

He springs the door of my cage open, scoops me out with one hand and holds me gently in both arms against his chest. He touches the back of my neck with his mouth and nose. I can feel his moustache against my fur and smell his dark human breath so close. He carries me outside where there's warm sunshine and he puts me on the front seat of his shiny black car, unharnessed and uncaged. I scoot my rear end over and look out the open window as he starts the car with a twist of his hand, the engine's low roar, the wind in my face and the blue sky soothing me as we drive away.

"Today we're going for a ride," Gazenko announced brightly. For a moment, I thought I was still sleeping, but I looked up and there he was, opening my cage and attaching the harness and leash. The other dogs had to stay put as he trotted me down the hallway into an enormous room where I'd never been before and strapped me tightly onto a little couch, which was attached by a long pole to a machine in the middle. I squirmed in every direction but realized I was trapped. He stuck wires to my chest and told me to smile for the camera. Then he closed the door and left me there alone. I heard the groan of the machine coming to life and I began to move. The couch went around slowly at first, then picked up speed. I was terrified because I'd never moved so fast; my heart was pounding in my chest. My weight sunk somewhere deep inside me and I grew heavier, until I could no longer breathe. Every part of me was sinking as the machine flung my couch around and the heaviness pulled my eyes and brain deep inside me, until all was dark. I no longer felt alive; I'd merged with the couch and we'd become a part of the whirling machine itself.

When I woke up back in my cage, the others whined to comfort me. Most of them had been taken for "rides" before, so they knew exactly what I'd just experienced.

"It always ends in sleep," one of them said. "That's the best part."

"There was nothing good about it, " I snapped back. "I thought I was going to die!"

"But you didn't," Albina whispered from the next cage, as if that made the whole event more palatable. At that moment I hated her, but didn't have the energy to tell her so. Instead I pouted and pretended to nap the rest of the afternoon.

Over the next few days, most of us were taken to what I'd begun calling the "torture room" often, where we went on different kinds of "rides," sometimes strapped to a platform that rose and descended so fast that part of you stayed behind, other times shaken unmercifully or whirled into unconsciousness. All the rides emitted horrible noises that stung our sensitive ears. Always death seemed eminent, just before we passed out.

Always when I'd wake up back in my cage, Gazenko would be nearby, watching intently. He was always nicer just after one of the rides. He'd greet me in a soft voice; he'd open the cage and scratch me under the chin, then he'd start poking me with his instruments, taking care to write down whatever he discovered.

I'd snarl, turn away from him and try to think even harder about how to get myself out of this place. I could not forget the story I'd heard about Smelaya. Whenever he'd come near me, I'd strain my nose, trying to detect unfamiliar dog scent on him, but since I never could, I'd nearly dismissed the story as rubbish: dog gossip they invented to entertain their pitiful little selves, I decided.

At the same time, I reasoned to myself, if there was even a tiny chance I could get out of here, shouldn't I pursue it? Of course I should. To do so would contradict my trusted instincts and require all of my concentration, but I decided that I'd become the best dog in the kennel, the only one worthy of Gazenko's attentions. If I could make him care for me enough, maybe he'd decide to take me home with him. I'd get out of this hellhole and my dream of freedom would become reality.

I decided not to tell the others about my plan, not even sweet Albina, who deserved better. If this was a competition, I needed to keep the advantage that secrecy would provide me. Smart, fluffy and beloved dog that she was, I knew Albina already had an edge over me; but I was sleek and scrappy, determined to do better, and confident I could perform whatever acts necessary in order to win this contest I'd just invented.

3.

Galina was up before Lilia; she'd dressed in a smart navy skirt and beige turtleneck sweater and had already made a pot of coffee when her sister lumbered groggily into the small kitchen, still wearing her white nightgown, topped by one of Victor's big sweaters to keep her warm. Galina jumped up to pour coffee for Lilia, who thanked her and sat down at the table, pleasantly surprised by her sister's unusual early morning ministrations. Galina, normally such a sleepyhead that Lilia had to rouse her each morning or else she'd be late to work, was wide awake, pacing restlessly around the small kitchen.

"Please, sit down," Lilia said, noting her sister's agitation. Then she asked, even though she knew she was not supposed to, "Do you have an important assignment today?"

"Make me look like you," was her sister's non-sequitur response, more of a question than a command.

"Impossible. You are naturally the pretty sister. I'm the plain one. Why would you want this?"

It was true that Galina had been blessed with wavy, copper-colored hair; Lilia's hair was duller and naturally straighter, and although she had learned how to curl it into a stylish coiffure, most often she pulled it back into a neat bun. Both women had pale, roundish faces and thin lips. Lilia was more adept at makeup, however; her lips were often full and red, and her cheeks rosy, while Galina had always been satisfied to let her natural beauty prevail — until this morning, when she'd suddenly decided a makeup session with her older sister was in order.

"Please, Lilia," Galina begged, perching in a nearby chair and taking her sister's hand. She knew exactly how to get her sister to comply. "I'm supposed to see Oleg... Dr. Gazenko today."

She watched smugly as Lilia got up without another word and opened a small cabinet below the sink, removing a worn shoebox and a hand mirror. She carried these items to the table and opened the box.

"Here." She handed Galina the mirror. "Now please turn yourself toward the window so I'll have more light."

Lilia lifted a compact containing face powder and another filled with rouge from the shoebox, then pulled a fresh white tissue from the pocket of her sweater. She went to work on her sister's face; Galina followed the progress, looking often into the mirror, murmuring her approval at each step of the process. Finally Lilia opened a tube of lipstick and twisted it until a flat red column emerged.

"It's nearly gone," Galina observed. "You need to get a new one."

"Hold still," Lilia busied herself getting the outline of her sister's lips exactly correct.

"Don't worry," Galina continued. "I'll get you some new lipstick later today, when I get off work. I'll stop on the way home."

"You don't have to do that," Lilia replied. "I can ask Victor for some money."

Galina admired her prettily made-up face in the mirror. "It will be my payment of your fee. Your work is high quality; you're a professional."

Galina carefully put the top back on the tube of lipstick and began packing her sister's makeup back into the shoebox.

"You can leave it out," Lilia said. "I was thinking I'd fix myself up this morning. I'm going out later."

"Out where?" Galina knew her sister rarely left the apartment alone. She said Victor wanted to know she was safe at all times. He didn't trust the streets below.

When her sister did not answer, Galina insisted, "If Little Sister can't keep secrets, then Big Sister shouldn't be allowed to, either. Come on, you must tell me."

Lilia was looking at her own pale face in the hand mirror, lifting her hair on one side, crimping it into a soft wave, smiling at the results.

"I'm going to confession."

Galina burst out laughing. "You haven't been to confession since mama made us go while papa was away fighting the war. You're suddenly remembering your religion?"

"You're right. It's been a long time. I must have a lot to confess!" Lilia laughed with her sister, making light of her intentions.

"And Victor?" Galina snickered. "Will your good Communist husband be confessing by your side?"

"You mustn't tell Victor any of this!" Lilia, suddenly anxious, moved to see her sister off to work with a quick good-bye hug. "Don't kiss my check. You'll ruin your lipstick. Now go have fun with this...Dr. Gazenko."

"You have fun yourself, with this...this priest." Still laughing, Galina threw her camera bag over her shoulder and left the apartment.

She stepped into the street, bracing herself for the morning chill, and trotted the block and a half to catch the Metro, where a businessman on the crowded train rose as she climbed aboard.

"Please take my seat, miss." He gestured toward the seat he'd just vacated.

Galina saw in his admiring eyes how attractive she must be today, thanks to her sister's makeup skills. Her cheeks burned with embarrassment to be suddenly noticed; she was more comfortable when she blended into the crowd, but she smiled sweetly and thanked the man as she sat in the seat he'd offered. She wondered whether she'd get the same reaction later today when she saw Oleg, and she began practicing what she might say to this very important man.

"It is good to see you again, Doctor Gazenko...I am so happy that you like my pictures... can you tell me more about the space dogs, such a fascinating subject...."

Then she admonished herself, "No, no, no, Galina, do not ask this man any questions...."

She must remember to smile and let him take the lead. Men were fond of quietly appreciative women like her sister Lilia, but this was not Galina's way. She had questions for everyone and was hard pressed not to ask them. How else could she find out what she wanted to know? She could tell, for instance, when her sister was keeping secrets, she mused as she rode downtown to the news bureau, and a series of questions popped into her mind. Why this uncharacteristic behavior? Have you gone batty? What if the good Communist Victor finds out you have returned to your religious roots? And what in the world would you, my pious older sister, have done that is worth confessing?

It would be fun this evening, Galina smiled to herself as her train reached its destination, to coax Lilia into confessing about her confession.

4.

They are trying my newfound patience, Gazenko and his assistants, and threatening to wreck my carefully cultivated good mood, which I have a hard enough time maintaining even under the best of circumstances. Yesterday and today, they have dressed me in one ridiculous outfit after another, as if I were a model preparing for a fashion show. The first was layered, a soft shirt and trousers (imagine, trousers on a dog!), then some sort of padded vest decorated with metal rings, which made me feel heavy and bloated. Then today they dressed me up again, but this time strapped a rubber bag to my rear end — surely not a fashion statement!

Gazenko himself sat me down in a padded seat just wide enough for me and my bulky outfit, and attached the rings on my vest to its sides so that I could barely move. I trembled as I waited for the noise and the shaking to start, but there was none. Instead, Gazenko told me to sit; I was barely able to accomplish this, with that butt-bag in the way. Then he said, "Stay," and walked away. Soon I heard a low whirring sound right in front of me; a paw-sized door opened and a lump of that disgusting food they give us suddenly appeared near my mouth.

Obviously this was some kind of a test. Was I supposed to eat the food or not eat the food? Which would please Gazenko more? Albina was not around to give her usual advice, so I sat quietly for a long time; then, when it seemed like mealtime, I politely swallowed the horrid food, without making a face. After that, I struggled to lie down gracefully, rested my head on my paws and tried to take my afternoon nap, but I couldn't go to sleep. I needed to poop. Usually I just squatted and pooped — preferably some distance from where I slept or ate. But now I had no choice, so I squatted right where I was. I could hear my turd plopping into the little rubber bag attached to me. Unfortunately, there would be no way for me to drag my butt across the ground to clean it, so I sat still for a while longer, feeling dirty and uncomfortable, but determined not to let it show.

Gazenko burst into the room.

"Kudryavka, you are a little marvel!" he exclaimed, unhooking me from all the apparatus. This time he kept me in his big arms, hugging me, brushing his face against my neck and ears. "Even the brilliant Albina will not use the bag for me," he whispered in my ear.

I had used the bag! Pooping into the bag, that's what this test had been about. I'd won this round easily, with an ordinary, well-placed turd; moreover, I'd made Gazenko happy with me. Try as I might to ignore it, I was feeling pretty cheery myself. Being nice to a human was not all that difficult; I stretched my neck up and licked him right on his big fuzzy moustache.

5.

A young woman in a white lab coat greeted Galina when she arrived at the kennel. Like the dogs, this woman had a name tag: she was Dr. Gazenko's assistant, Korinna.

Korinna ushered her guest into a private office, where Galina was told to wait. The doctor, Korinna explained, was completing his afternoon check of the dogs and would be here shortly. Galina sat for a moment in the sturdy wooden chair on one side of a big metal desk. On the other side was a leather chair where Dr. Gazenko would sit, so worn that its padding showed. A few neat piles of paper were stacked on the desktop, some typed and some handwritten; she was sitting too far away to read any of them. None of your business, anyway, she chided herself.

Then she got tired of waiting and decided to take a self-guided tour of the little room, which ended quickly because there were not many decorations or furnishings to examine. She studied a stiffly-posed photograph on the wall behind his desk of a younger Gazenko wearing an army uniform, his insignia revealing officer status, perhaps a lieutenant; next to it, his diploma from the Second Moscow Medical Institute, framed cheaply and hung just a tiny bit off kilter. Galina's strong aesthetic sense urged her to straighten it, but she knew she should not touch anything in this office. After being reprimanded by her boss yesterday, she was determined to be on her best behavior here.

One small window with no curtains opened onto an outdoor space contained within tall chain-link fencing; it looked like a prison yard. There was more brown than green there, as if constant trampling had worn away all the grass, leaving only the bare dirt, and in the shaded corners, a few white patches of old snow. Small wooden buckets were situated haphazardly, each filled to the brim with water. She liked the way the sunlight glinted off the surface of the water, and without really thinking of it, she pulled out her camera and snapped off a few frames, stopping when she heard footsteps in the hallway.

"We take them out there twice a day for exercise," a soft deep voice behind her said. "It's good for their little canine systems."

She turned to take Oleg Gazenko's offered hand and shook it, then sat again in the wooden chair while he took his seat behind the desk. She rested her hands in her lap, smiled and waited for him to initiate conversation, an uncomfortable few moments.

Finally he cleared his throat and asked, "You have brought your photographs from yesterday?"

Happy at last to have something to do, Galina pulled her camera bag to her lap, removing a brown envelope from it. She remembered to smile again, but he did not notice. Perhaps she should get down to business.

"Yes. Here are the pictures you asked to see, sir."

As she spread her photographs out on the desk for him to examine, Galina felt herself relaxing into her professional manner. She had to admit to herself (though never to her sister) that she was just no good at flirting. She believed she could make a much better impression using her intellect and showing off her photographic skills. Like now.

"Yes, yes, yes," he kept saying each time he picked one up and held it in the window light to examine it. "At first, I thought you were a reporter with all your questions, but now I see the truth: you're a fine photographer."

"I apologize for asking so many questions," she said quietly. "That was not my job."

"That's nonsense," he replied, "for how else will you find things out?"

She couldn't help it. She smiled broadly. He grinned back at her. Of course he'd noticed how her hair was styled today and her makeup perfectly applied; she was young and quite beautiful. He did not spend much time around well-groomed females; scientific women tended to dismiss such niceties in their determined quest for knowledge.

"So you must not be shy here," he encouraged her. "Are there any other questions you have? If so, please ask." He waited.

"Could I...would it be possible to see the dogs again, even maybe to shoot more photographs...."

She listened to her own nervous voice trailing off before she could get one coherent question out. Silly girl, she chided herself. This visit is not going well at all.

But within minutes she was in the kennel, Gazenko by her side. As if he were not such an important man, as if he had all the time in the world, he patiently opened each cage, pulled each dog out, sat her on the table and introduced her to Galina. Then, in his best authoritative voice, he commanded the dog to "stay" while Galina moved about and shot multiple photos of each one.

Of course I knew what *stay* meant and so of course, when Gazenko lifted me from my cage and sat me in front of this visitor, I behaved. This was my new routine. I not only sat and stayed, I cocked my head, curled my ears and tried to put on my prettiest face for this woman, who held a funny black box in front of her own pretty face and made it click over and over.

"Have you chosen the space dog yet?" I heard her ask him suddenly, from behind her box.

"Not yet, but there are a few under serious consideration," he answered, glancing at me. "At this point, I cannot tell you more."

Quick as a fox and quiet as a rabbit, Galina saw the look he gave me; coughed and clicked. Gazenko did not notice.

Then she smiled and thanked him for his time.

"Perhaps you'd like to see the new photos when I have them ready," she suggested before departing.

"Of course I would," he replied, "but please remember — you don't need an invitation. You are welcome to visit us any time."

Korinna, the white-coated assistant, entered the kennel then and offered to escort Galina to the front door.

"You look very nice today," Korinna remarked as she led her visitor down a long hallway.

Galina judged them as being about the same age, though Korinna was shorter, wore thick eyeglasses, used no makeup, and her badly permed hair was a frizzy mess. It's like she hadn't looked at herself in the mirror this morning, Galina mused. Maybe she hadn't had the time. Maybe she didn't have a mirror. Galina experienced a brief moment of guilt over her own luxurious preening earlier this morning.

She thanked Korinna and felt bad at not being able to return the compliment ("you look like an unkempt, near-sighted poodle" would not be nice). Perhaps some other small talk was needed.

"You must enjoy your job here," Galina said, "working with the dogs every day."

"I like this job very much," Korinna turned and smiled, then continued in more of a whisper, "and I love the little dogs, almost as much as Dr. Gazenko does."

"He seems so serious and professional," Galina remarked, "yet you say he is a dog lover as well?"

"I think sometimes he considers this a flaw. He cares so much about the dogs that he gets upset when one of them has to leave the kennel."

"Don't they all leave eventually? I mean, they are being trained for scientific work, are they not?"

Korinna had reached the front door of the kennel. Without a pause, she flung it open for Galina.

"I believe your bureau has a car waiting for you," she smiled a sincere farewell.

In the back seat of the sedan driving her back to the news bureau, Galina puzzled over the way Korinna had ignored her question about what happened to all the dogs. Undoubtedly this information was classified. Maybe not all of them were successfully trained. Maybe the workers at the kennel found good homes for the ones who did not succeed. Maybe the worst would not happen to these failed scientific dogs, she shuddered, but who could say? Even for human beings who were locked away, there was no guarantee of ever coming home again. Her own papa, and Lilia's, an automobile mechanic who'd brought some parts of the German culture back with him after the war — German automotive magazines and his favorite German cigarettes — had been arrested soon after he returned home. The knock on the door had come early in the morning.

"It's nothing," he'd said to his wife and small daughters as the *cheka* took him away. "It's a misunderstanding and will be cleared up soon." He'd smiled and added, "I'll see you all at dinner tonight."

But the extravagant dinner their mama spent the whole day preparing, a small ham punctured all over with clove sticks, baked potatoes with real butter, homemade bread and creamed cabbage, went uneaten. After Galina and her sister had set the table, their mama told them to sit on the sofa and wait, while she paced the small living room, looking often from the window as night fell, as the food grew cold and bedtime grew near.

"What did our papa do wrong?" Galina had dared to ask. Their mama composed herself into a tall proud statue and answered her daughter with the single word, "Nothing."

Of course her answer offered little comfort to the sisters' girlish souls. Why would the *cheka* come for you if you had done nothing wrong, Galina had been desperate to ask, but she'd stifled herself. The girls fell asleep on the sofa; they never saw their papa again. Convicted as a traitor (evidenced by his possession of German cigarettes and magazines), he'd disappeared into the gulag, and had never re-emerged.

6.

Lilia crept down the back stairs while Victor was busy cleaning the bakery kitchen as he did at this time each afternoon, always a noisy process, plus he kept the radio on full-blast and often sang along with it, believing himself to be a fine operatic tenor. She'd put on what she considered her most flattering dress, a peach-colored floral print she'd sewn herself, with a round collar and full skirt, underneath her solemn gray winter coat. Once outside, she hurried not to the front door of the church, but to the side door where the priest lived. It was half past three in the afternoon. She paused for a moment, then knocked lightly.

"You have missed today's confession," the priest spoke through the narrow crack he'd opened in the door. He was not inclined to open it any further. Like most Soviet citizens, he did not like surprises appearing at his door.

Lilia was afraid he was going to close the door again, so quickly she pulled a small waxed paper package from her coat pocket and thrust it through the crack in the door. "Here," she said, "it's a day old but still delicious."

The priest opened the door a little wider to see the baker's wife standing there, the full skirt of a very fancy dress hanging beneath her drab overcoat. Her legs were sheathed in black stockings and she shifted her weight nervously on tiny feet nestled in shiny black pumps. Why had she come here, dressed like this?

"Forgive me for coming unannounced, Father, but I bring news you'll be happy to hear."

"It's a fruit tart you have brought me," he noted, a little puzzled, unwrapping the package, but still keeping the door between them. He was appreciative about the tart, but he had no idea what to do next. He could not be in the habit of inviting married women into his private quarters.

"Thanks to you, and to your husband, and may the Lord bless you both for this kindness," he attempted.

"May I come inside, please?" Lilia was persistent. She'd planted herself there at his door, the brisk autumn wind swirling around her legs and skirt.

He could not leave her outside in the cold. He opened the door all the way and gestured her inside, shutting the heavy wooden door behind them, hoping no one passing by had seen her enter.

"I thought perhaps we could have tea again," she prompted him.

"Yes, of course," he agreed, grabbing his kettle, filling it with water, lighting a burner on his old gas range and slightly burning himself in the process, the whole time lecturing himself silently and praying without knowing whether the Lord would offer guidance in situations like this. He watched as his guest made herself comfortable, removing her coat, sitting delicately on the edge of his narrow iron bed and crossing one leg over the other, revealing one stocking-ed limb nearly up to her knee.

Was she flirting with him? The kettle whistled then, so he served the tea and then settled himself uneasily in his rocking chair.

"Who is that?" Lilia pointed to a picture hung on the wall, the smiling man in a black outfit topped by a tall black hat with a wide brim.

"I'm not sure of his name," the priest told her, "but in America he's a famous cowboy. I saw him once in a movie."

"Is he evil?" she wondered out loud. In the few American westerns she had seen, the bad men always wore black.

"No, he's a very good man," the priest replied. "He's especially kind to children."

"I see. And over there is Jesus."

Nailed to the opposite wall, Jesus, smiling and glowing in white robes and topped by a sparkling halo, made the sign of the cross with one hand and held an ornate book in the other. She could read from its open pages: "Love one another as I have loved you."

"Yes, another very good man," he laughed.

"I am surrounded by very good men!" Lilia observed with a pretty smile. Her teeth were white and straight, her lips a luxurious red.

The priest shifted uncomfortably in his chair. This small talk was maddening because he did not understand its significance. Why was she here? What did she want him to do? When would she leave and did he even want her to?

"What is this news you have for me?" He proceeded cautiously. Surely, no evil would come of this conversation; he could not allow it.

"I think I know where to find the little dog," she smiled.

Over a hot mug of tea, Lilia told the priest about her sister going to take pictures of the government's dogs at the Institute of Aviation and Space Medicine.

"I'm sure our little stray is there," she concluded.

"Did you see her in your sister's pictures?"

"I saw dogs much like her. I'm sure it's only a matter of time before we find her. My sister is there again, this very day."

"This is of great concern," he opined, and Lilia vigorously nodded her head in agreement.

"What do they do to the dogs there?" she asked.

"Some kind of scientific experimentation, I suppose." They both sat silently contemplating the worst that might happen.

"I wonder," Lilia finally said, "whether our little dog will survive. Do you think it's proper to pray for a dog, Father?"

The priest offered a silent prayer of gratitude. The Lord had provided him a way to manage this situation.

The woman had come to him for spiritual advice, something he could offer with confidence.

"Of course we can pray for her. St. Francis teaches us to pray for all living creatures."

"That's a great comfort for me, Father," Lilia smiled with sincerity, "but what if she does not survive, Father. Do you think she will go to heaven? Do dogs have souls?"

"Again, St. Francis believed all living creatures to have souls, and to have an afterlife."

The priest advised Lilia that they should both agree to pray morning, noon and night for the well-being of the little dog, he in his room and she in her apartment over the bakery.

"Our prayers will converge as they ascend toward heaven," he told her, pleased that he'd been able to respond to the spiritual needs of this lovely woman without succumbing to the corporeal temptation, while feeling undeniable warmth beneath his robe at the very thought of their future, conjoined prayers. He wished he'd put on undergarments this morning, but he'd rinsed his only pair last evening and they were still not dry. He rearranged his robe to hide evidence of his warmth, and hoped, for the sake of both their souls, she'd get the message that she shouldn't come back here alone.

Lilia, who knew exactly how long it took Victor to clean the bakery kitchen, close the shop and come upstairs, suddenly panicked.

"I must go, Father," she jumped up. "I wish I didn't have to run...."

Surprised, yet relieved her improper visit was about to end, he rose to see her to the door.

"That's all right. Please give my regards to your husband," he told her as she hurriedly left the rectory.

The priest stood in the open doorway, welcoming the rush of cold air swirling around his feet and rising beneath his robe to surround his thin legs and his groin. Sometimes, he mused, a knock on the door is not the worst that can happen. And still he had a fruit tart to enjoy!

As he watched his visitor run awkwardly away from him in her high heels, a soft glow surrounded him and an uncustomary smile crept across his face.

Nearby, an unseen observer watched them both until the woman disappeared into her own doorway and the priest finally stepped back inside and closed the rectory door.

7.

Vincent had finished his work early. He was waiting in the apartment when Lilia returned, sitting stiffly at the kitchen table.

"Where have you been?" His voice was low and controlled. "You didn't tell me you were going out."

Lilia's heart was pounding; she thought quickly and replied, "I needed a new lipstick." I've just lied to my husband, she realized.

"Let me see this new lipstick," he growled, anger creeping into his voice. "How much money did you spend?"

"They were out of my shade," she explained. I've just lied to my husband again, she thought; I shouldn't be doing this, but she continued nonetheless. "I'll have to go again tomorrow. Perhaps you can accompany me. If not, I'm sure Galina will go with me."

"That bitch sister of yours!" He was shouting now. "She's the one who puts dangerous ideas in your stupid head. She should not be living here!"

Moving rapidly for all his mass, Victor rose from the table and lunged toward Lilia, catching her by one ankle and pulling her to the floor. He turned her over to face him, crawling up her body, pinning her down with his own. Trapped underneath his bulk, she could hardly breathe.

"I want her out of here," he hissed into her face. "If you don't throw her out, then I will."

"Please," she moaned, closing her eyes tightly. She didn't want to see what might happen next.

"Please what?"

"Please don't hurt me," she begged in a tiny voice.

He thought for a moment, than rolled off her slowly.

"If I wanted to hurt you," he said more calmly, "you'd already be dead. Believe this."

His rage subsided as quickly as it had erupted. He stood himself up, but did not offer to help her up. He lumbered to the toilet and closed the door. She opened her eyes when she heard the stream of his urination. She pushed herself up on her hands and knees and crawled toward the bedroom. Her new stockings were ruined; she removed them both and crawled under the covers.

When Galina came home a little past six that evening, Victor was nowhere to be seen and her sister was already in bed, complaining of a headache.

"Can I get you some aspirin?" Galina asked, but Lilia shook her head no.

"What then? Will you get up if I warm you some soup?"

"I'll help you with the food. You've been working all day long." Lilia moved the quilt covering her and slowly sat up, dangling her bare feet over one side of the bed. She had on her new dress, Galina noticed, and just below her pretty skirt, one ankle was marked with a fresh, dark, ugly bruise.

Galina gasped. "What happened to you?"

"I took a fall," Lilia answered quickly, "trying to hurry too much down the back stairs. One board is loose, you know." This lying was becoming easier the more she practiced. She stood unsteadily and started toward the kitchen. "Don't worry, I'm all right."

The sisters sat quietly enjoying the warmed up borscht Lilia had prepared as last night's meal. Galina found half a loaf in the breadbox. There was no butter to put on the bread, so they both dipped it into the soup bowls to flavor it. Soon Galina felt a question coming on.

"Where's Victor?" Her brother-in-law rarely missed an evening meal. "Something is wrong, I think. So please, you must tell the truth."

Lilia stopped eating and sat looking into her soup for a long time before replying. "Victor," she said, "wanted me to ask you when you will be getting your own apartment."

"That's nonsense. He knows as well as you do that I'm on the wait list, but it could still be several months. And that does not explain your damaged ankle any more than falling down the stairs. I seem to remember that Victor fixed the loose board last week, did he not?"

"Do you remember," Lilia continued thoughtfully, "how we had so much fun with make-up this morning? And how happily we both anticipated this day?"

"Yes," Galina waited for more.

"That time," Lilia pronounced, "was long, long ago." She would say no more.

After dinner, Galina insisted on washing and drying the dishes all by herself. Then she put her sister to bed and gave her valerian drops to help her sleep before settling herself on the living room sofa. She could not sleep; this business with Victor, who'd still not come home, was troubling Galina. She knew her brother-in-law did not like her. She didn't like him that much, either. She'd much rather live alone and had been looking forward to getting one of the government apartments, even a tiny studio with only room for a bed and table. But now she did not think she should leave Lilia alone with him, though refusing to leave might make Victor behave even more badly. What to do?

"It will come to us," their mother used to assure her daughters when they were so frightened that they could not think what they should do to keep themselves safe, warm and fed properly from one day to the next.

She wished fervently that their mama was still alive, to tell her daughters how they were supposed to survive their lives, even though she had not survived her own. Soon after receiving news that her husband had been executed, she'd herself had died, unable to bear the sorrow. The sisters, still teenagers, had raised themselves the rest of the way, Lilia cooking, sewing skirts and knitting sweaters for both of them, cleaning and taking care of whatever small room they could find to live in, and Galina working her way through high school and vocational training to provide the income that would have to be enough to support them.

Then Victor had come along, already the proud owner of a small bakery, an established business with private living quarters above it. He had an eye for the older one, Lilia, and began courting her; within a year, they were married, all three of them, it seemed, as Lilia had sworn never to abandon her younger sister. Victor reluctantly agreed they could all live in his little apartment — temporarily. He'd hoped, for the first few years, that his sister-in-law would catch herself a husband, but she rarely went out with boyfriends, and lately he'd sensed that even his wife had given up on her younger sister ever finding a suitable man. No wonder, Victor thought, with that brassy personality of hers. He'd put up with them both because he had to. But now, with all the new construction downtown and with her new job, they all knew Galina was eligible for her own apartment.

Any day someone might call to say one had become available, and she would have to be ready with an answer. Galina knew herself to be much better at questions than answers. If her horrible brother-in-law dared show up here again, she'd ask him, "What do you think you're doing with my sister, who loves you so? Why can't you behave yourself? Why can't you control your temper?"

But when she heard her heavy-footed brother-in-law stomping up the stairs, making enough noise to wake the whole neighborhood, she lost her nerve, quickly turned out the light and pretended to sleep.

8.

Oleg Gazenko drove himself home at the end of another long day. He was in agony over the decision he'd soon be forced to make. The necessary surgery needed to be scheduled, and during the final days of intensive training, he must devote his time to just the space dog and her designated backup. He didn't know the date yet they'd have to travel to the launch site. No one knew, but whenever The Chief Designer contacted him, he and the dogs would have to be ready to go within a day's notice.

Of course he'd already thought a great deal about this decision and he knew which two dogs should most logically be selected. One of them was perfectly behaved, an experienced rocket dog, and pretty enough for the press she'd get. The other one, a newcomer, seemed inexplicably to have trained herself to obey his commands, and her system had adapted effortlessly to the diet, the confinement and even to the tortuous testing on machines. She was easily the most physically fit, and though she wasn't as pretty as the snowy white one, he'd come to adore the odd markings on her face, her long, pointed nose, and her shiny dark eyes barely disguising the attitude he knew she still possessed; he sensed her remarkable efforts to keep herself under control and admired her greatly for it. In the end, this space dog job was all about maintaining self-control.

Inwardly he moaned; he was doing it again, growing too fond of the dogs. It will be a great honor for this dog, he reminded himself, to serve her country in such a glorious way, just as it is a great honor for me to prepare her for this mission. He knew himself well enough to predict this emotional behavior — he'd done this just before each of the low-altitude rocket launches — but he seemed unable to control it. A huge lump had filled his throat each time he'd closed the dogs into their rocket carrier, not knowing whether he'd ever see them again. He'd mourned for days after each disaster, and celebrated with the dogs that had returned safely from their adventure. Once, as he greeted a returning dog still shivering from fright in his arms, he knew in his heart that he could never put this terrified little creature through any more training. He told his staff she was too high-strung for this kind of work. He took her home with him; she was there to greet him this evening, a honey-colored dog with one floppy ear, skidding on the linoleum floors in her rush to greet him, always as if she'd thought she'd never see him again.

"Hello, Smelaya."

She was an old dog now; she'd flown more than six years ago, and white hairs were beginning to crowd the golden brown fur around her snout. He fed her dinner, real dog food, not the special food they fed the dogs at the kennel, then took her out for their evening walk. Even though the wind was chilly, he was careful to move slowly; the dog suffered these days from arthritis. Smelaya's unsuitability for the stressful rocket dog work and all her acting out had, ironically, ensured her survival well into old age, while the well-trained and well-behaved space dog, whichever one he would choose, was destined to die soon — most likely within days.

Once home, he was not hungry for his own dinner, so he went to sleep without it; Smelaya curled up in a soft basket next to his bed. Before lying down, he sat on the edge of his bed as he did every night and wound his alarm clock, set, as always, to wake him at four a.m. The ticking clock on his nightstand reminded him that time was running short for all involved in this space mission, but especially for the dog he must choose, the first one who would live — and die — in outer space.

There are so many ways a dog can die young, he tried to console himself. She can run in front of a speeding car. She can soil the rug and be beaten to death for it. She can choke on a chicken bone or wander into the forest and be eaten by wolves. At least this dog will die a glorious death and everyone will know of her sacrifice. She will become famous and beloved throughout the world.

He knew how the Soviets managed their publicity — if they wanted the world to know about you, there would be no end to the reminders: photos in the newspaper, interviews on the radio and newsreel footage shown in movie theatres. On the other hand, if they did not want the world to know who you were, the photos would be retouched and the film edited until you'd disappeared; in fact, you'd never even existed. Even the important Dr. Gazenko could not yet predict whether he actually existed in the photographs the pretty young photographer had taken of him. His visibility was yet to be determined by his future performance; his work ultimately would be judged by the all-powerful Soviet propaganda machine.

Before it was too late, before any airbrushing could commence, he decided he would ask the young woman for a photograph of him with the dog, a secret picture he'd keep with him always as a reminder of his growing affection for the dog he'd be forced to choose: the smartest one, the healthiest one, the skinny one with the curly tail.

9.

The next morning, Victor baked tarts and muffins as usual, arranging them under the glass domes on the counter. He'd slipped back into the apartment late last night, careful not to disturb his sister-in-law sleeping on the living room sofa. She'd be gone soon and he wouldn't have to tiptoe around so. Lilia was sleeping soundly in their bed; he'd undressed to his shorts and undershirt and had lain beside her, whispering in her ear that he was sorry, that he loved her so much, that the thing he'd done would never happen again. He couldn't tell whether she'd heard or not; she had not stirred. He must remember to tell her this again, when she was awake and their lives were back to normal.

"Good morning," the barrister who worked in the office next door greeted Victor as he entered the bakery, jingling the bells on the door. The two men barely knew each other — Victor didn't know his neighbor's name and doubted the barrister knew his — even though they saw each other almost every morning and Victor knew what baked goods to gather without being asked.

"And how are you this beautiful day?" Victor asked, grabbing his tongs to lift two warm, golden muffins from the display and wrapping them in wax paper for his customer.

"I'm fine, thank you," the barrister replied, pulling his wallet from inside his overcoat. As he removed two bills and offered them to Victor, he continued, almost as an afterthought. "But I've just heard some disturbing news."

"Yes, and what would that be?" Victor answered, encouraging his mysterious neighbor to linger. The barrister lowered his voice and made careful eye contact as he went on.

"I've heard that there are citizens among us who do not support our leader Khrushchev and his bold efforts to take us into outer space."

"How could this be?" Victor was incredulous. "After the wonder of Sputnik, what Soviet citizen wouldn't want another victory such as this?"

"It's hard to believe," the barrister nodded in agreement, putting his wallet away, but still watching Victor solemnly, "yet I'm glad to hear this disturbs you as well."

"Of course I'm disturbed," Victor replied, "but what can we do?"

"In my line of work," the barrister explained, "the best course of action is to find these individuals, have them arrested, and bring them to justice before they can damage the Soviet Union."

"And that's where you come in," Victor looked to the barrister for confirmation.

The barrister nodded, toying thoughtfully with the goatee on his chin. "Yes, this is the work I do."

Finally he looked away. He'd answered Victor truthfully; this was his line of work, but his work had become much more complicated under the new Party leader, who seemed determined to please the elite as well as the masses. Sometimes the speeches Khrushchev gave made him swing like a pendulum, first pledging to reform and diversify the Soviet legal system, then circumventing this same system in order to re-affirm the waning influence of his secret police, whenever necessary to assert his power and maintain control. In the past year alone, Khrushchev had released millions who'd been arrested under Stalin from the gulags, but at the same time he'd had thousands more incarcerated because he and his police considered them "dissidents." The new prisoners wanted justice and fair trials. The released prisoners wanted exoneration. Barristers like himself were caught in a fluid legal system that made the actual practice of law nearly impossible.

Article 58, the section of the Soviet criminal code that had permitted such easy incarceration and conviction for suspected subversive activity during the Stalin years, seemed far less relevant these days than when it was first passed in 1934, yet, still on the books, it *was* the law. There was a specialized new police force, formerly the *cheka*, now called KGB, working directly for Khrushchev and the Central Committee to enforce laws prohibiting political dissent and subversive activity, while the job of the regular police force was now limited to non-political law enforcement of civil and domestic crimes such as burglary, assault and public drunkenness. Civil law, the basis of his profession, was now only applicable to those arrested by the "regular" police, while political justice, an area of increasing interest to him, was limited to KGB control.

But, the barrister mused to himself, what if someone drunk on the street expressed anti-Soviet sentiments? Which police should be informed? What if someone committed a burglary that somehow compromised the progress of the Soviet culture? Under Communism, isn't a crime against one individual also a crime against our entire society? It was the gray legal area that intrigued him most and at the same time frustrated his efforts to make a living. He'd taken to writing his own interpretations of such cross-over Soviet legal areas, hoping to make sense of them, perhaps someday being praised for his astute interpretations and possibly even being elevated to a high judicial position within the Party, but always locking his notes inside his desk at the end of the day. One could ill afford to openly express his opinion on the government, on the law, on crime and punishment, until the appropriate sentiments were known and stabilized. Until then, one had to remain ever vigilant, circumspect in his own activities and also in those of his neighbors.

"How is your wife?" the barrister asked the baker.

"She's fine. I will give her your regards," Victor answered, pleased to pause and chitchat a little longer with this man who normally kept his distance and had little to say.

"You are happy in your marriage?"

"She is the perfect companion; we are very much in love," Victor replied, wondering momentarily why the barrister had asked, but another question followed in rapid order, dismissing his concerns.

"And the other young woman who lives upstairs, that is her sister?"

"Yes, she has a good job, working for TASS," Victor bragged. "So much success she will be getting her own apartment soon."

"You must be pleased for her."

"Yes, yes," Victor grinned, "pleased very much for her, for me, for us all!" The two men laughed heartily and the barrister departed, knowing a little more about the baker and his family than he had known before.

Back in his office, the barrister wrote of his conversation with the baker, filling several sheets of paper before locking them away in his desk drawer, sighing, and leaning back in his chair to examine the ceiling.

10.

One thing Victor would never have revealed to the barrister, even if asked, was the fact that he'd locked his wife inside the apartment when he'd left for work this morning, to keep her safe, he reasoned. He was not proud of himself for doing this, but had done it anyway. Surely Lilia would understand his concern.

Lilia had pretended to sleep as Victor got up, dressed and left the apartment. She listened for the sound of the apartment door closing; then it would be safe for her to get up. But she heard an extra sound, another lock clicking. She waited a few minutes, then tiptoed to the door and tried the knob. It was locked and the key, which usually hung on a nail beside the door, was missing. She looked everywhere for it, not wanting to admit what she suspected, that her husband had made her his prisoner. Why couldn't he just ask her to stay home during the day; she'd do it, wouldn't she?

She looked at the clock ticking on the kitchen table. Seven o'clock, still early in the morning. Victor wouldn't come home before four, and Galina's hours were unpredictable. She looked out the window at the deserted street below. There was no one to help her.

Then she remembered the priest and their commitment to pray for the little dog; she realized she'd no longer be alone if she joined with him in prayer. She dropped to her knees and began praying earnestly, and not only for the dog, but for herself as well. She had not prayed in a very long time and struggled to find appropriate words.

"Please, God." She repeated these words when she could think of no other ones. Surely the all-powerful Lord would know what she was praying for and could fill in the blanks. Surely sincerity counted more than voicing the proper words.

She finished her prayer, turned on the radio and increased the volume. A plodding and predictable speech by some Party official burst forth, but she did not care what what was on, as long as she did not have to listen to her husband singing today. She sighed and decided she might as well scrub the bathtub and toilet; she removed a wash bucket from underneath the kitchen sink and filled it with soapy water.

Downstairs, the bakery door jingled open and the priest entered, wearing his wide-brimmed black hat.

"Hello, Father, and good morning to you," Victor greeted his customer.

The priest removed his hat, walked purposefully to the counter and smiled at Victor on the other side.

"I came to thank you very much for your kindness."

"You are most welcome," Victor was trying to remember this kindness the priest was speaking about.

"For the tart you sent to me yesterday."

"Of course, for the tart."

"Your wife was kind enough to bring it to the rectory."

"I see. My wife came to the rectory?" Victor repeated the priest's words, struggling to put yesterday's pieces together in his mind.

The priest realized the baker had not known about the tart. His ruddy cheeks turned redder as he hurried to correct any misassumptions.

"Of course you must know how concerned she is about the little dog that's missing."

"I know how fond she was of that dog. What a pity, yes?"

"I've advised her to pray," the priest answered. "That's really all we can do, yes?"

Lilia had just finished cleaning the bathroom when she heard the key turning in the lock. The door opened and Victor burst inside the apartment, strode to her and pulled her into his arms.

"Please don't," she begged. "I'm a mess."

"I'm sorry," he whispered. "I didn't know you were upset about the little dog."

Lilia, surprised and frightened, didn't know how to respond; the smartest thing, she decided, would be to remain silent.

"I will get you a little dog if you want a dog," he continued. "I'll ask around to see if anyone has a litter. I'll go with you to pick one out. You will have a sweet little puppy dog."

Still Lilia did not respond. She was afraid to tell him she didn't want just any puppy dog; she wanted the one she'd already chosen, the one who had disappeared suddenly from the street below. She closed her eyes and let Victor hold her and kiss her repeatedly. Her prayers, her patience and this careful silence she was cultivating, she reasoned, would keep her safe.

11.

A black-and-white image emerges from the watery chemicals, ghostly at first, then darker and crisper. The doctor is smiling, but he does not look toward the camera lens, rather at the white dog with the unusual facial markings posing next to him.

"Hello, Oleg." Galina smiled at the doctor in her photograph; she'd caught the moment, a significant one.

She pulled the dripping print from the development tray and held it close to her eyes, straining to see the details under the soft orange light of her darkroom. She quickly finished the process and hung this print up to dry. Then she hurriedly printed another one, identical, anxiously watching the door to make sure she was not disturbed. She was only supposed to print one set, unless instructed otherwise.

Close-ups of the dogs hung on clotheslines all around her. She'd made duplicates of each. As soon as they dried, she'd present one set to her boss, and would surely be praised for her talents. She'd keep the other set for herself; if discovered, she would say these were for Dr. Gazenko. For now she would hide them, stuffed in an envelope she'd put under the darkroom supply cabinet; this evening she'd smuggle these out in her purse and take them home to show Lilia. Her sister could tell her if the little dog from her neighborhood was among the dogs she'd photographed today at the kennel.

There was more on her mind. Once Lilia had identified the dog, Galina was planning a surprise; she'd ask Dr. Gazenko to give her the dog to take home as a companion to her sister. If dogs could leave the kennel, why wouldn't he approve this plan? Galina would have to be charming when she asked this; she'd wear her best outfit and she'd flirt determinedly. A dog, even a small one like those at the kennel, could be trained to protect her sister as well as to keep her company. Then Galina could move to her own apartment without worrying so much about Lilia, home alone with Victor. They'd all have what they wanted; it was a perfect plan.

Galina had predicted her boss's reaction correctly. When she took the set of prints to his office, he marveled over each and every one.

"These close-ups are extraordinary," he exclaimed over the dog portraits she showed him first.

"If you look carefully at this one," she told her boss then, handing him the photograph she'd taken of Gazenko with the dog called Kudryavka, "I think you can see something quite interesting. See how he is looking at this little dog?"

"Yes, he seems quite enamored by this skinny little mutt. Why do you suppose he looks at the dog this way?"

"I can't be sure," Galina offered, "but I think perhaps he's chosen her to be the space dog."

"Please make me more prints of this one," he instructed her, "and any more you have of this dog only. If this is correct, we must be ready when the news is announced."

Late that evening, Galina spread the second set of photographs across the kitchen table, where Lilia sat, picking up each one, holding it beneath the overhead light and staring intently at the dog in it. She kept returning to one, then proclaimed: "This is the dog!"

"Are you certain?" Galina asked.

Lilia nodded her head vigorously. "I'm sure of it."

"Well, then, look at this." Galina pulled another photograph from the big envelope in her purse and handed it across the table to her sister.

"Your little dog is called Kudryavka," she continued. "Here she is with Dr. Gazenko."

"Yes, that's definitely her," Lilia smiled at the dog in the photograph. "So she's all right?"

"She's fine," Galina grinned. "I think Oleg is taking extra good care of Kudryavka."

Though her sister begged for details, Galina would say no more.

"I'll find out more very soon," she told Lilia. "Until then, you must be patient. And you must tell no one. Not Victor. Not anyone."

For the first time in days, Lilia went to sleep beside her husband, feeling hopeful about what tomorrow might bring. On the living room sofa, Galina lay awake, anticipating the next few days: so much would happen so soon; she must be ready.

12.

My plan to become lovable was working well. I'd stopped acting out and Gazenko was responding nicely to my charms. I'd begun to look forward to his visits, since now much petting was involved, plus treats. He'd reach inside my cage and smooth the hair on my back for no reason at all. His touch was gentle and I responded by licking his fingers, one at a time; this made the solemn doctor laugh out loud.

I'd even taught him a clever trick. He'd hold out a treat, dangling it just a little higher than my head. I'd bark once, the signal that he should lower the treat so that I could grab it with my mouth. He'd also learned to smile at the end of each food transaction.

I was let out more often for exercise in the fenced-in yard next to the kennel, a virtual garden of delights: dirt to roll in, sometimes fresh snow to sample, but most thrilling, a reasonable sized area to run around in; I'd dash back and forth, the rarely used muscles in my legs rippling with excitement. Several times I tried digging a hole, remembering the story of Smelaya's escape, but someone always saw me and called me away before I could make much progress in the frozen ground. If the others had any sense at all, they'd be helping me with this; we could dig secretly, in shifts, some of us distracting the humans while others kept up the digging. I always tried to signal them whenever we were taken out for exercise, but usually they were too excited to pay attention; frolicking was the only thing on their little minds.

We still had to endure the torture room, at least Albina and I did. For some reason, the other dogs had been given more time off (certainly not for good behavior!), while Albina and I were worked even harder on the noisy machines. Gazenko had chosen us both for special treatment; now he spent nearly all day with the two of us, leaving the poodle girl Korinna to babysit the rest.

I knew what this meant: Albina and I were the finalists in this contest to win his affection, while the other dogs were no longer contenders. Just as I'd predicted, the pretty white dog was providing my stiffest competition. I'd have to work harder.

Early this morning, when he'd come in, I'd decided to do my Albina imitation, jumping up, whining, wagging my tail and pawing the front of my cage in what I considered a grand display of my adoration for the man — so over-the-top that Albina and the others sat wide-eyed and gawking. They'd never seen me behave this way.

He opened my cage and smiled at me as usual, though not quite as broadly.

"Oh, Kudryavka," he mussed my fur and scratched my ears. "What's gotten into you?" He lifted me out of the cage and cradled me in his arms, but did not look me directly in the eyes. He seemed distracted; I sensed a note of sadness in his voice, so I wiggled my head around to lick his face. I whined a response to him: *don't worry, I'm fine*. This didn't cheer him up at all.

He carried me into another room with painfully bright lights overhead and strapped me down on a cold table. I don't remember what happened next, but I woke up in agony. I was back in my cage, lying on my side, and I could barely lift my head. There was a big, uncomfortable collar surrounding my neck and chest, only I couldn't move my head enough to see it, and I couldn't get my paws up there to scratch it off. The other dogs were alert, except for Albina, who was sleeping in her cage, but when I asked them what had happened, they claimed ignorance.

"You two were taken away," one of them tried to explain, "and then you both came back to your cages while you were still asleep, but you had those white collars around your necks."

I looked over at Albina and saw what they were talking about. She was lying on one side, eyes closed, one of her front paws twitching uncontrollably, her neck surrounded by a thick white bandage that stretched down her chest and around her front legs, wrapped so tightly that she'd hardly be able to move. Like me.

So many questions crowded my brain. If this was special treatment for Albina and me, what did the humans have in store for the others? How much more special was my life going to get? How could I possibly pretend to be nice to any human who treated me like this? What would sweet Albina do? I barked in her direction. I wanted her to wake up right then so we could talk, but she could not be roused.

Back in his office, Gazenko picked up a fountain pen to write some notes on what he'd just done, but his hands were shaking and he had to put the pen back down on his desk. He'd barely been able to hold them still during the surgery sessions, one for Kudryavka and another for Albina. He could no longer delay the inevitable. He had to prepare two dogs for the bioinstrumentation, two dogs because the chosen dog must have a backup. One at a time, he'd put them to sleep long enough to open up the neck, exteriorize the main artery, wrap it with skin, and then sew the wound back up, leaving the exposed artery looped outside the dog's neck. Just before launch, he would wrap the exposed artery with a small metal cylinder containing a bladder that could be inflated and deflated; this would enable him to monitor the dog's blood pressure during the space flight.

He'd also cut four tiny slits in each dog's chest, one under each armpit, one at the top and another at the bottom of the breastbone, and had inserted tiny silver electrodes, which would be wired to devices in the dog's travel compartment that would monitor heartbeat and respiration. He'd implanted two more at the outer edge of each eye; these would record the dog's brain activity and eye movement during periods of sleep.

He'd not only made his decision; he'd acted on it. There was no turning back. He felt a jolt of sympathetic pain in his own neck and chest, stood and forced himself to take several deep breaths.

Someone knocked on his door. He'd told Korinna that he needed time by himself, to catch up on his paperwork. She should not be disturbing him without a good reason.

"Yes?"

Korinna opened the door a sliver. "The lady photographer has brought you more photographs. Should I tell her to come back some other time?"

He thought for a moment before answering.

"It's OK." A pleasant diversion may be just what the doctor needed.

The door opened fully and the lady photographer pushed past Korinna, strode confidently toward him and offered her hand first. She was even prettier than before, in a smart gray suit with red velvet collar and trimming. A tiny red hat sat perfectly on her well-coiffed hair. Her lips and cheeks were rosy and her green eyes sparkling.

It was all show; inside Galina was petrified when she considered the trouble she could get into for this unannounced visit, even though, in an imaginary conversation, she had cleared it with her boss. In fact, he had encouraged her to deliver the extra photos she'd printed to Gazenko, and to try to find out for sure about the space dog. In her fantasy, it was permitted to ask questions.

"Hello, Dr. Gazenko," she said, shaking his hand. "Forgive my showing up here unexpectedly, but my boss insisted I show you the photographs I took during my last visit. I was hoping he'd called to let you know I was on my way."

"I've been busy this morning," he explained, "no time to take phone calls."

"Of course." She remembered to smile again as she shuffled though her purse to retrieve the envelope holding the photographs. She regretted that she was perspiring inside her best outfit, which would be difficult to clean. This flirting was difficult work.

"I'm pleased to see you, and the photographs. I think you have read my mind. I was thinking of calling to ask for them myself, Miss...." He realized he did not know her name.

"I am called Galina."

"And I am Oleg to you."

So far, so good, she thought to herself. They were on a first-name basis already. He praised her photographic talents once again, and asked whether he could keep this set.

"Yes, of course." Galina took a deep breath. Her official business accomplished, she would have to leave soon. She learned forward in her chair. "Oleg, I wonder if I could ask you a question?"

"I thought we'd already determined that asking questions was encouraged," he smiled at her.

"The dogs here, can they ever go home? I mean, they cannot all go on space flights, so can the ones who do not fly be adopted? Or the ones that do fly, do they ever retire, with permission to live elsewhere?"

"These are many questions you are asking, so before I answer, I must ask you at least one," he responded. "Why is it you want to know such things?"

"It's for my sister," she explained earnestly. "I live now with her and her husband, but will be getting my own apartment soon. My brother-in-law works hard all day, and my sister will be lonely. If I could give her a small dog, this would make her very happy."

"I see." He was noncommittal. "For your sister."

"I owe her everything," Galina continued, the pitch of her voice rising. "Without her help, I would not have survived. I would not have been allowed to learn photography. Our parents, they died when we were still young girls, our father in a gulag."

He nodded, but did not respond, so she forced herself to go on.

"And now my sister's husband, he provides for her, and I think he must love her very much, but he also has a bad temper. I think a well-mannered little dog like the ones I've seen here might help calm him down after I've moved away."

She knew she could say no more. She'd said too much already. She'd told him private things she should have kept to herself.

He leaned forward across the desk and took one of her hands in his. He noticed her hand was trembling. He stroked it to ease her nervousness, just as he'd learned to do with his dogs.

"A little dog for your sister may be possible," he told her. "You are a good sister, to be so considerate of her needs."

Galina allowed herself a deep breath before she continued, "I'm wondering about the little dog called Kudryavka, if it might be possible..."

He cut her off. "But today is not a good day for adopting a dog."

Korinna mysteriously reappeared in the doctor's doorway to escort Galina to the front door of the kennel.

"I'll call you at the news bureau," he assured her as she left his office. "We will try to do something. For your sister."

"We're very busy," Korinna apologized as she led Galina down the corridor.

"Preparing for the flight of the space dog?" Galina ventured. She thought she saw Korinna nod her head, so she pushed on. "It will be a proud day here when the little dog returns from her space flight. Perhaps I will be able to come and take more photographs."

Just as they reached the entryway, Korinna stopped short and turned to face Galina, a stormy look in her eyes visible behind the big eyeglasses.

"You take pretty pictures," she hissed in a low whisper, "but you understand nothing about the space dog."

She pulled the door open and waited for Galina to exit.

"What do you mean?" Galina stood there stubbornly. "What will happen to her?"

Korinna shot another powerful glance at her. "Shhh." She put her hand on Galina's back to gently push her outside, and shut the door behind her with a polite slam.

13.
Baikonur Cosmodrome
October 25, 1957

The noisy sky had become silent again as the batteries aboard the orbiting Sputnik 1 ran down. The incessant beep, beep signal had become weaker, then intermittent, and finally, this morning, had ceased altogether.

Just as well, Number 20 thought when one of the scientists who'd been monitoring the satellite brought him the news. That's one less distraction to interrupt my work.

In the assembly building, the powerful R-7 rocket, modified to lift the heavier payload into space, and the four boosters, built and transported as separate modules, were now all connected in a massive cluster. The whole thing rested horizontally on a flatbed rail car, awaiting completion of the third stage, which would be attached to the payload. Once the third stage was in place, the launch vehicle would travel the short distance on railroad tracks leading to the launch site, tail first, and would then be raised into its vertical position and connected to the support towers for final checks and adjustments, for fueling, and for the final payload preparations, including the insertion of the canine passenger.

In his role as The Chief Designer, Number 20 had personally supervised nearly every task completed at the Cosmodrome, hurrying from building to building, from room to room, from detail to detail. The pace was frantic; he was exhausted, but disciplined enough to keep his mind sharp and focused on whatever activity was in front of him, and his overwhelming to-do list had grown a little shorter each day.

This morning he'd announced he would work in solitude in the space room; he needed the quietness to concentrate on his final check of the payload capsule, testing every instrument, every device, every connection. At the end of this, another long and exacting workday, he hoped he would be ready to place the crackly, long-distance phone call to the Kremlin, the one Khrushchev had been expecting.

"Yes, sir," he'd say. "All is well here, we are on schedule to launch the first week in November, just before the holiday."

He knew that with this communication, he would have committed himself and his workers. He had to be sure. He could not fail at any step in the process. He was sure about the R-7 rocket and its boosters; now he had to be sure about the payload. Only after this rigorous and thorough check, which he trusted to no one but himself, would he be ready to send the telegram to Dr. Gazenko at the Institute, three terse words, "We are waiting," prearranged code which meant, "Come and bring the dogs within the next 24 hours."

Organized scientist that he was, he approached his task one step at a time. First he checked the instrument mounted at the very top of the spacecraft, a relatively simple spectrophotometer to measure any ultraviolet and X-ray signals encountered on the space flight. Next he turned his attention to the familiar shiny ball still resting in two halves, containing the batteries, measurement devices, radio transmitters and the new telemetry system that would function for the first time during this space flight. Tral-D had not been ready for the first Sputnik, and he had not been sure it could be functional in time for this launch, but his engineering crew had come through for him, for them all. With Tral-D, Number 20 and his ground tracking crews would be able to receive extensive information about conditions both inside and outside of the spacecraft. Moreover, they would know intimately the dog's vital signs — heartbeat, blood pressure, respiration rate, even when she ate, slept and dreamed.

Just yesterday, an enormous problem had been solved quite simply with an ordinary alarm clock. The sheer volume of information to be handled by Tral-D would quickly deplete the spacecraft's limited battery supply system. One of his assistants had come up with a way to set the clock and connect it to the telemetry system so that transmissions would be limited to 15 minutes out of each 90-minute orbit, timed to coincide with the spacecraft's path over the Soviet Union. This, thought Number 20, was the kind of brilliant, fly-by-the-seat-of-your-pants thinking that he and his crew were known for. Good work, he'd told this assistant, and now here is another problem for you to solve. At the Cosmodrome, as it had been at the Design Bureau, the award for inventiveness was always another nearly insurmountable task to be tackled, and there was never time for rest, relaxation, or well-deserved revelry. The prize, he'd tell them, would be the successful launch of the rocket and the orbiting satellite carrying the first space passenger.

"When you hear the first bark transmitted from space," he'd say, "then you may celebrate."

That bark would come from inside the canine container, all in one piece now, at first glance impossibly tiny even for a small dog, but Gazenko's tests had proven that dogs could adapt to its confines. The "cradle" where the dog could sit, stand or lie down was luxuriously padded on the bottom and sides; the dog would be adequately cushioned during the explosive launch; there were also springs and a neck brace to protect the dog; these would be retracted once she became weightless. Miniature hooks and chains from the passenger's vest to the walls of the cabin would keep her in place, and sensors attached to wires implanted in her chest and head would transmit her vital signs to the Tral-D, which would record them, and then during the 15-minute transmission period during each orbit, relay them back to Earth.

If anything went wrong, the tracking crews on Earth would find out, once during each hour-and-a-half orbit; in fact, during these periods of transmission, they would know far more about the condition of the dog and her spacecraft than she would know herself. At all other times, they would know nothing at all. There was an odd remoteness to the whole procedure, displaced as it was in both space and time. He wondered whether the dog would be able to sense how absolutely alone she'd be for most of her journey in space.

All the earlier rocket dogs had traveled in pairs; the scientists agreed that two made more sense than one. If one should die, perhaps the other would not. If one became ill or decided to act out, the other may not. Always it was better scientifically to have comparative data. But by design and necessity, this first space dog would travel solo; they could not afford the extra weight. This fact had elevated Gazenko's role as the scientist who would select and train the space dog — so much depended on his judgment, and this was the one part of the mission over which Number 20 had the least control.

He was understandably anxious for the doctor and his dogs to arrive. Number 20 needed to see for himself that the first space dog had been well prepared; her performance was vital to the success of everything else on his final checklist, beginning the moment she entered this travel cabin, which seemed to be in perfect working order; he checked "done" on his list.

There was one more new instrument for this Sputnik, untried and untested, a slow-scan television camera to record moving images of the canine passenger, using the Tral-D system to relay the pictures to Earth. Images of dogs in flight were nothing new; in most of the sounding rockets, workers had mounted a 16mm movie camera to film the dogs, then retrieved and processed the film once the rocket had landed. Filming this space dog was not an option, however, since the satellite would not be returning, so Number 20 had made a bold decision to incorporate a "space test" of this brand new television technology.

The camera was mounted just above where the dog would ride in the canine cabin. Number 20 stuck his head inside the cabin, turning to position himself precisely where the dog would travel, and looked into the camera lens for a good long time. When he removed himself from the dog's container, instead of checking the camera mount off his list, he stood quietly, becoming increasingly melancholy about the dog's eventual fate. All care would be taken to insure a painless death; this he had guaranteed Dr. Gazenko, but he had not realized until now that if all went as planned, if the new television camera worked properly, they would not only be able to watch the little dog live in space, but also see her die there, one hundred lines in each picture, ten pictures each second, the most amazing, troubling television show ever.

"You perform incredible feats and yet no one knows your name. No one sees your face. It's as if you are invisible," Number 20 remembered someone once lamenting.

Visibility, he decided, should not be the goal after all. Better to live and die without the whole world watching. Why should the little dog's fate be any worse than his own? With that, he loosened one connection on the television camera, guaranteeing its eventual failure, and completed his final check of the payload with his signature on a piece of paper authorizing his workers to move the payload to the assembly area and attach it to the rocket.

What he'd just done was improper and uncharacteristic of him, a strict professional, but this was the reasonable and humane thing to do, to assure the passenger privacy during her final moments. The vibration caused by the launch would most likely completely disconnect the television camera before the spacecraft ever reached orbit, or soon after, and no one would suspect tampering. Death with dignity, he reasoned, was the least he could do for the little dog who would be giving up her own life for the success of his space program.

14.
Moscow
October 27, 1957

The unusual proclamation came suddenly over Radio Moscow from the Soviet leader Khrushchev himself!

"Our scientists and engineers are making preparations to launch a new Sputnik into orbit around the Earth. This event will commemorate the fortieth anniversary of the October Revolution. Coming so soon after the great success of our first Sputnik, there will be no doubt as to the Soviet Union's vast superiority in outer space exploration.

"There will be another amazing thing about this upcoming launch. Our scientists and doctors are now preparing a team of dogs for space travel; one of these dogs will be onboard the next Sputnik as the first living passenger ever to rocket into outer space."

The Soviet leader concluded by promising more revelations about the upcoming launch, very soon.

"You will hear from the space dog and her trainer, here on Radio Moscow. Please stay tuned," the announcer added. Then there was a musical interlude.

"Amazing news," the barrister said as he stopped by to purchase his morning muffins, and Victor enthusiastically agreed.

Plans to launch the first Sputnik had been shrouded in secrecy. No one knew until after it had happened. If the launch had not been successful, there would have been no news issued, as if the launch had never been planned, and no pictures published, as if the rocket and satellite had never existed. *Pravda*, the Communist Party newspaper, had run a very small notice in its October 4 edition about the launch of an artificial satellite; the Party was still not sure this news was relevant. After the world's enthusiastic reaction, however, the same newspaper ran a much longer story the next day. Visibility only upon Party approval. Celebration only after that. Even after the announcement on Radio Moscow and then the full story in the next day's newspaper; even after the beep, beep, beep it emitted; even after ordinary citizens had run outside at dawn and dusk to scan the sky for a glimpse of the shiny object; still it took awhile for the Soviet citizenry to realize the importance of what had happened. Now, quite uncharacteristically, they were being told in advance.

"The scientists must be very confident about this trip into outer space, or else they would not have told us until its success was assured," the barrister explained to Victor.

"What could happen?" Victor laughed.

The question ran like a loop in the barrister's mind, even after he'd left the bakery and returned to his lonely office. Because there was no immediate answer, the question continued its relentless torment throughout the day and into the evening.

15.

Now that I was feeling a little better, I had to re-think everything. What had all my over-the-top fawning gotten for me? A headache that wouldn't go away and a wound that wouldn't heal. Whatever Gazenko had done to me while I was asleep had left a big raw bump on my neck. I could see that Albina had the same bump, an ugly blemish on her pretty white fur. The fur had been scraped away, and the skin that was left was red and scabby. She didn't complain, of course. She never would. The doctor knew what was best for us, she'd explained, and I was growing tired of arguing with her.

"Relax," she'd tell me. "It will be all right."

But I sensed something different. The mood at the kennel had changed dramatically; no more fun and games. Every time Gazenko and Poodle Girl came in to check on us, they were glum and silent. I thought I'd caught Korinna weeping one morning, but when I looked closer, she brushed a stray poodle hair out of her eye and smiled broadly as she stuck a thermometer in Albina's rear end, then in mine.

It was only the two of us now. Albina and I had been separated from the others and I had to wonder whether I'd been wrong about the contest; maybe we two were the losers. Maybe the others were running free this very moment, chasing cats and peeing on fire hydrants.

The door opened. Gazenko entered, forcing a smile in my direction.

"Kudryavka, remember the trick we learned?"

He opened my cage and gently lifted me out. He set me on a bench and pulled a treat from his pocket, holding it just a little higher than my head. I barked and he lowered the treat until I could grab it in my mouth. Beef jerky.

"That's a good girl," he smiled on cue, this time, it seemed, sincerely. He'd brought one of the little outfits they liked to dress me in, a red jacket that covered my chest and most of my neck.

"Now come with me," he said, pulling the jacket over my head and fitting it in place, careful to cover the wound on my neck. "We have some visitors who'd like to meet you."

The phone call this morning had come as a complete surprise. Khrushchev was preparing to make a public announcement on the radio about the space dog. TASS had been instructed to "interview" the soon-to-be famous dog. Could they come to the Institute this afternoon?

Gazenko hesitated before answering. He'd become more protective of both Albina and Kudryavka since their final days of training had begun. He could not afford to stress the two dogs any more than absolutely necessary. So much depended on their good behavior, and he knew how easily a slight unsettling in the canine nervous system could result in uncontrollable acting out.

"Can you tell me what you have in mind?"

"Perhaps a small press conference with you and the chosen dog?"

"No cameras!" he'd replied tersely. The dogs still had scars from their surgeries. The public should not see them this way. They would not look like heroes.

"Then how about a radio interview? One microphone only, how would that be?"

Gazenko nervously had agreed to this plan. He was not at all sure Kudryavka would be cooperative today. He'd sensed a slight edginess in her the past few days. Nonetheless, he'd filled his lab coat pocket with treats and had gone to prepare her.

Now he smiled his big public smile as he carried the dog into the room where several men were waiting. One walked up and pointed a microphone in Gazenko's direction, while another stationed himself in front of them, watching his wristwatch as he held one hand up in the air. Behind him, a third man, wearing earphones, worked the recording deck.

"Stand by," the man with the wristwatch said, and then he lowered his hand briskly. A red light from the recorder blinked on.

"We are coming to you direct from the Institute of Aviation and Space Medicine," the man standing next to Gazenko spoke into the microphone. "It is here that important work has been going on, to train a dog to fly into space. We have the dog's trainer here, and we have the very special dog who has been chosen to become the world's first space dog. He is small, no more than six kilograms, I'd say, a little scruffy around the ears, white with brown markings, a mixed breed, I believe. And he's wearing a fashionable red vest! What is this dog's name, doctor?"

"This dog is female," Gazenko politely corrected the announcer, "and her name is Kudryavka."

"I see. And do you think Miss Kudryavka would say something to our radio audience?"

"I believe she might." Gazenko pulled a treat from his pocket and held it above the dog's head, anxiously waiting for her to take the bait.

When she heard the dog bark on the radio in her kitchen, Lilia jumped up and yelped in amazement. Victor heard it downstairs on the radio he kept on in the bakery, and cheered. The priest sitting in his chair in the rectory heard it and thought of the little dog who'd disappeared from the neighborhood and of the baker's wife, whom he'd thought of each time he'd offered a prayer for their missing dog.

Galina and her co-workers at TASS heard it; they'd gathered around a radio earlier, anticipating this announcement. The news bureau had sent the radio crew now interviewing Gazenko and the dog. Galina was pleased to hear Gazenko's voice as much as she was pleased to hear the dog bark. She'd thought of him often since their last meeting and wondered when she'd see him again. Of course she'd approached her boss earlier today to ask whether she could go along for the radio interview.

"I'm sorry, but no," he'd replied. "The doctor made it clear there should be no cameras today. So much the better to have the photographs you took on your last visit."

She'd been right, of course. The dog Gazenko had introduced to her that day as Kudryavka was in fact the dog who'd just barked to radio audiences everywhere.

"Excellent," Galina's boss had laughed out loud when he heard the dog bark. "We knew this already, about this Kudryavka, did we not?" He winked at Galina. "Please send the photographs out now." She turned to do what she was told.

In his office next to the bakery, the barrister also heard the bark on his radio, and in a sudden epiphany, he knew the answer to the baker's question: what could happen? Of course the safety of the rocket and its satellite would not be compromised — he knew someone would be watching it every step of the way from Moscow to the launch site, and every moment from the time it was constructed until it blasted off into space. In contrast, the little mutt might seem much less valuable. He wondered whether anyone would think to arrange security for the dog? How easily might she be snatched from her keepers and spirited away before she got her chance to fly into outer space? Who might be inclined to do such a thing?

Thinking feverishly now and tapping one foot nervously on the floor, he unlocked his desk drawer, pulled out his notes and reviewed them. Ha! This Kudryavka who'd barked on the radio was the name of the dog the women upstairs had talked about so often; suddenly he realized the danger may be close at hand. What he'd assumed at first to be a domestic matter may in fact be a subversive plot designed to undermine the Soviet space program! It may be required soon that he put on his other hat, the furry *ushanka* he wore when doing surveillance for the secret police. It may be required that he save the dog, in order to preserve the integrity of the upcoming Sputnik mission. He may be the only person who knew enough to put all the pieces together, and what he knew, if he acted on this information quickly and wisely, might be enough to make of him a Soviet hero.

Part Three

Testing

1.
Moscow
October 29, 1957

There was no doubt; I'd won the contest!

The sign on my tiny cage still said "Kudryavka," but ever since we'd performed our trick in front of the man holding the metal stick (he'd kept calling it "radio"), Gazenko had been calling me his little "Laika" (that means "barker," remember?). Indeed, he was so pleased with our performance that he petted me at length before returning me to my cage that day. Of course Albina was still around and she was treated with the utmost courtesy, but I'd clearly outdistanced her as Gazenko's favorite. I tried not to lord it over her; I'd even begun to feel a little sorry for my fluffy little friend; she had to sit and watch the grand displays of affection he continued to offer me daily. I think she'd been top dog in this kennel forever, and now she had to play genteel runner-up to this upstart newcomer, me. As usual, Little Miss Sunshine accepted the situation graciously.

"You deserve to be the favorite," she told me when we woke up this morning. "You've worked so hard, and in such a short time you've accomplished so much."

She still lived next door, so conversations were easy, though our cages were impossibly small, and seemed to get smaller each day. These days, even turning around, as all dogs love to do before settling down, was out of the question. There were no more outdoor romps, either; I was feeling claustrophobic and more than a little anxious.

"So when do I get out of here?" I asked her. I was sick and tired of the strict confinement and more than ready to go home with Gazenko and live with him forever.

"I think we will leave very soon now," she said, and my doggie brows shot up in surprise.

"What do you mean, 'we'?"

Albina sighed and sat down, preparing one of her patient explanations.

"It will be like what happened to Kozyavka and me," she told me. "You and I will leave the kennel, take a long trip, fly in a box with fire underneath, float down to the ground, and then come back here to celebrate over a fine dinner — no gray mush, real dog food."

She seemed pleased by the prospect, but I was severely annoyed. That's not the contest I'd entered and now, apparently, had won. The grand prize was supposed to be unconditional freedom.

"I don't want to come back here," I snapped. "Not ever!"

Albina's words had set off a growing sense of foreboding in my gut. My situation was not exactly what I'd thought it to be and I didn't know for sure what was going to happen next, but I sensed that some response was required.

So I decided to howl. I lifted up my head, opened my throat and let the sound escape from deep inside my chest. I made such a beautiful sound, I kept on howling. There was a melody that pitched itself way up and then down, and a rhythm that stretched one note out nearly forever, then pulled the same note back with several pointed bursts, the volume adjusting itself to match the pitch changes for maximum sonic impact. And I wasn't doing a thing to control it; I just sat there, listening in delight as the musical composition arranged itself in my throat and the sounds poured forth.

Quizzically, Albina cocked one ear and listened for a while, then she joined in, subtly at first, then she let herself go, providing deep and resonant backup to my lead. I suspect she'd never before let it rip like that. Looking back over those final days, that was the best time the two of us ever had there. For a few minutes, I forgot I was in a cage, and I'm pretty sure Albina did, too. Our voices had no boundaries, and neither did our little canine souls. Instantly we'd become wild, uncontrollable, running free in our minds, and there was no stopping us until *we* decided it was time. Korinna the Poodle Girl came in and tried to shush us, then called Gazenko. He sized up the situation correctly, led Korinna out of the room and left us to our primitive selves.

"It's all right," I heard him tell her. "They need to do this now."

Eventually we wore ourselves out and settled down again, glowing inside with satisfied fulfillment. Albina's little pink tongue was hanging so far from her mouth that it grazed her prim white toes. Her dark eyes still danced to the impromptu song now lodged in her soul where she could surely find it again, even without my guidance. This howling I'd shown her was pure instinct; it's not something you learn, like rolling over or sitting up for a treat, and the reward comes from the act itself, not from some kennel-keeper.

"What was that all about?" Albina wondered.

"If you have to ask," I told her authoritatively, even though I'd just figured it out myself, "it's not something you need to know."

2.

A light snow was falling, just beginning to dust the streets and sidewalks. Inside the apartment, Lilia pulled on her boots and buttoned herself into her winter coat.

"I'm only going as far as the Metro stop," she assured Victor, explaining that she must go to meet her sister because Galina would be carrying extra equipment and would need her help. Victor pouted slightly but didn't protest. She'd left a big iron pot of cabbage soup simmering on the stove and told him to help himself if he didn't want to wait for her and Galina.

"Maybe I'll do that," he said. She set a bowl and spoon on the table in front of him and he grabbed her as she passed, pulling her to his lap and kissing her hard on the mouth.

"You are still my girl, yes?" he asked, grinning, and she answered him softly, as she always did these days, "Of course I am."

His touch alone terrified her, but she'd taught herself to mask her fear with a quick smile. Tonight, however, Lilia's smile hid more immediate matters demanding her attention. She was certain Galina would bring news of the dog who'd barked on the radio earlier this afternoon, and she could not wait until Victor went to bed to find out all her sister had seen and done today. She hurried toward the train just arriving and was relieved to see her sister stepping carefully onto the thin snow carpet, struggling to balance her purse and her camera bag.

"Did you see her?" Lilia reached for her sister's purse. "Do you have more photographs?"

"I wasn't allowed to go," Galina answered, handing over her purse and rebalancing the heavier camera bag.

"Why not? I thought you were welcome there."

"Not today — he said 'no photos.'"

"Why no photos? That doesn't make sense." Lilia was distraught. "Can you go there tomorrow?"

"No, I can't just go there any time." Galina sounded a little annoyed.

"Why not?" Lilia demanded.

"Something is happening there," Galina explained. "They've become very private. I think there are secrets we are not supposed to know."

The sisters made their way across the fresh snowfall already worn into slush by the rush-hour crowds near the Metro, then turned onto their own relatively deserted street, where the snow collected more evenly. Theirs were the first footprints to disturb its integrity.

"But Kudryavka, she's all right, isn't she? You said the doctor was taking extra good care of her. I heard her bark on the radio this afternoon. She's going into space? Did you know this before today? Why didn't you tell me?"

Lilia's rapid-fire questions were urgent, and when Galina did not answer right away, Lilia grabbed her sister by the arm of her coat and shook it. "Please, no secrets," she begged. "You have to tell me what you know."

As they trudged back to the apartment, their boots marking a clear path in the snow for anyone who cared to look, Galina huddled close to her sister, whispering everything she knew, and in addition, everything she suspected. She no longer believed the dog would survive her journey into outer space, and this knowledge had become too big a burden not to share. She rolled out the evidence mounting in her brain and presented it to her sister: the strange behavior and the cautious warning from the doctor's assistant, the sudden secrecy around the kennel, the specific refusal for more photographs to be taken there, the doctor declining to discuss Kudryavka's future, the fact that he hadn't called her since then even though he'd promised he would. The sisters stood in the street outside their apartment, under the bakery awning to keep the snow away from their faces, crying and hugging each other, then trying to rearrange themselves and their moods before going upstairs to face Victor.

"We can't tell him we're upset about a dog," Lilia whispered. "He would never understand." Galina nodded her agreement. Both sisters forced smiles onto their faces and marched upstairs to their apartment.

By now, another set of footsteps had formed in the fresh snow; a man in an overcoat and furry *ushanka* had followed the tracks made by the sisters on their street, had slipped into his office next door and now stood in the dark by his slightly open doorway, watching and listening. The barrister had heard enough of their conversation to know they were up to no good. These two, in his estimation, had become dangerous, perhaps subversive. Someone should inform the husband before they went too far. Surely the good baker would appreciate this information, if not all its implications. Perhaps, the barrister thought as he considered the hard evidence only (stolen government property — the photographs Galina had recently brought home from the news bureau), the wife might still be spared.

3.

Korinna knocked lightly on Dr. Gazenko's office door, and when he invited her in, she handed him the telegram that had just arrived. He tore it open and realized she was waiting to find out what it said. He nodded silently, then added, "The dogs and I will need to leave tomorrow. Can you be here early to help me with final preparations?"

Korinna bit her lip and replied, "Of course, sir."

"Why don't you go home now," he suggested. "Get some sleep. You look tired."

But Korinna did not move; she stood in place and her body become quite rigid as she spoke.

"Dr. Gazenko, sir, may I please go with you and the dogs? You may need help with them and they trust me as they do you."

"I'm sorry, Korinna," he told her. "There is strict security there and you have not been given clearance. Only myself and Yazdovskiy."

"You know Kudryavka does not like Dr. Yazdovskiy," she replied. "She'd behave much better around me. Perhaps I could still get clearance?"

When he shook his head no, she slumped into a chair and began to cry, silently at first, but then with loud gasping sobs. When he could bear to listen no longer, Gazenko got up from his desk and put his arm around her shoulders, trying to comfort the poor girl. Of course this is why she could not go, but he could not tell her. Korolev had insisted there be no women at the launch site; he did not trust women to control their emotions in stressful situations, and right here, in Gazenko's arms, was indisputable proof. That is why he had only requested security clearance for himself and for the Institute administrator to whom he reported, Dr. Yazdovskiy.

When she'd calmed down a little, Korinna stood and loosened herself from the doctor. She removed her eyeglasses and wiped them dry on her white smock before putting them back on. Finally, she brushed and smoothed her smock before speaking again.

"Then perhaps, sir, I could stay with the dogs tonight? That way I'd be here in the morning, as early as you'd need me."

"That's not really necessary," he answered. "Actually, I was planning to stay here tonight."

He'd just decided to do this himself. The impact of what was about to happen had hit him suddenly, as it had Korinna, in the gut. The dogs, he realized, should be given every grace possible during these final hours. Especially his little Laika.

Korinna had begun weeping again as he ushered her out of his office.

"It will be all right," he told her, a lie and they both knew it.

Now he listened to her footsteps in the hallway. Just as he'd anticipated, he heard the door open to the room where Laika and Albina were kept now. Despite his urging her to leave, he knew she wasn't going anywhere tonight.

4.

Victor had finished his meal by the time the sisters arrived at their apartment. He'd left his empty bowl and spoon on the kitchen table, so Lilia hurried to clean up his mess while Galina quickly changed from her business outfit into more comfortable clothes; slacks, a sweater and bedroom slippers.

"Where's the man of the house?" Galina asked as the sisters sat down to bowls of warmed-up soup Lilia had just put on the table. Lilia gestured toward the bedroom; Victor's snoring was just becoming audible as he settled into his usual deep sleep.

"Sorry, I'm not hungry tonight." Galina pushed her soup away.

Lilia removed both bowls from the kitchen table, emptied their untouched soup into the big pot on the stove and rinsed the bowls and spoons in the sink.

"I'll make tea," she suggested instead and her sister nodded silently.

"Isn't there anything we can do?" Lilia asked Galina a few minutes later, as they sipped strong tea. There was no cream to add to it, but neither sister thought to complain.

"Oleg will not part with this dog; I've already asked him." Galina rested her head in her arms on the table. "I can't come up with anything else. I'm trying, but everything I think of seems too risky."

"Like what?"

"Things we could never do." Galina looked up into Lilia's face and was moved by the desperation she saw there. "Things," she whispered, "that might mean we could not continue our lives as they are now."

Lilia considered the gravity of her sister's pronouncement before answering in the quietest voice she could use and still make herself heard.

"I think," she said, "that would not be the worst thing for me."

The snoring from the next room inched up several decibels, as both sisters considered all they may have to leave behind if they continued with such crazed and necessary thinking.

5.

Korinna made herself a little nest out of quilts on the floor beside the two cages and settled down to go to sleep. She was so close to the dogs she could hear their soft, even breathing. They'd been given light sedatives with their evening meals to make sure they'd get a good night's sleep. When Gazenko had realized she was not going to leave the dogs tonight, he'd made a pot of tea for Korinna and himself. It was all right to stay, he'd told her. He'd sleep on a cot he'd put in his office.

"Thank you, sir," she'd said, relaxing as she sipped her tea, soon yawning as fatigue overtook her hard-working body. She removed her eyeglasses and lay down on the quilts; she was asleep within moments.

Now as she slept soundly, a shadowy figure entered the room, stepping cautiously around her in the dark, going directly to the cage where Kudryavka slept, leaning over to open it, gently removing the dog so as not to wake her, and tiptoeing away.

6.

I'm always grumpy when I first wake up, and this time was no exception. Plus, it was the middle of the night, not a proper waking up time at all, I complained to myself. Right away I noticed the movement, noise and vibration, plus a chilly breeze moving across my wet nose. I sniffed the air for some familiar sign, but everything smelled brand new to me. I looked around for Albina, but she was not there. I was alone with Gazenko and he was driving me in a car!

He looked over at me, where I crouched anxiously in the front seat, and smiled.

"Take it easy, Laika," he told me. "We're going for a ride in the country."

If I was awake now, this was good news indeed. He removed one hand from the big steering wheel, cupped it over my head and scratched me behind both ears. Then he pointed out the window and I struggled, still groggy from sleep, to raise my head high enough to look out. Everything was moving past so quickly, all I could see was a blur of black above and another blur of white below. Then I lay back down to think about this, but I must have drifted back into sleep. These are untrustworthy times, the periods between sleeping and waking; you can never be sure what's real and what's not.

Eventually he turned the big wheel; I heard gravel crunching underneath us and we stopped moving.

"What do you think about this, my little Laika?"

I put my front paws up on the window ledge and looked out again at the night sky and the snow that covered the ground. It was not snowing now; in fact, the stars had come out, sprinkling themselves generously across the dark sky. The city lights glowed softly in the distance. I'd never been this far from home. I could not believe any of this, so I barked to convince myself this was real. My curly little tail nearly wagged itself off. I hopped from the window to Gazenko's lap and he held me there, stroking my head, fondling my ears.

"It's a beautiful night, don't you think?" he asked me.

For once, I wished I could be human; I wanted to answer him with real words, like the ones he used. I wanted my own hands and fingers to return his caresses, and big lips to plant kisses all over his face. Instead, I did the best I could with what I had, licking him endlessly with my wet tongue, pushing my nose close against his face, curling up in his warm arms.

If I was still asleep, I wanted this dream to last forever.

7.

Oleg knew he was behaving recklessly, but felt unable to control himself. When he'd realized Korinna was going to spend the night in the kennel, perhaps continuing in her agitated emotional state, he'd put a sedative in her tea, thinking this would not only be the best thing for her and for the dogs, but also that it would allow him to have unrestricted time with Laika, from now until morning, when they'd both have to put on their proper faces and leave for the Cosmodrome.

When he'd gone into the room where Korinna, Albina and Laika were sleeping, just to check on the dogs, impulsively he'd opened Laika's cage to stroke her back, but instead had lifted her into his arms. He stood there holding the sedated dog, sleeping soundly, and thought to himself, I should really do something nice for her now; she doesn't have much time left. The next thing he knew, they were in his car. He turned the heater on to warm them up and wrapped his overcoat around her before placing her on the car seat beside him. Shivering in his shirtsleeves, he drove quickly away from Moscow.

When she opened her eyes and looked at him, his heart nearly broke. He pulled off the road and shut down the engine. He must locate his self-control — where was it? He realized he'd been about to open the door, let her jump out and run away if she wanted. She wouldn't be the first dog to escape from the kennel. No one would suspect this was a deliberate act on his part. Maybe she'd find a pack of wolves to live with; he was sure she could hold her own even with the wild creatures that he knew roamed these woods. He'd heard her impressive howl this afternoon.

But then what? He'd have to turn to the pretty white understudy, Albina, even though she'd understand, as she had every other time he'd placed her in a rocket. Once, her rocket had overshot its target, going so high that it took her several hours to parachute back to Earth, hours during which he suffered and nearly died a thousand deaths, wondering how she'd ever survive the prolonged journey.

From his own wartime aviation experiences, he knew that every time you went up, there was an equal or greater chance you might not come down again, at least not in one piece. He'd witnessed so many crashes, heard so many sirens, inspected so many charred remains, that he should by now be inoculated against such visceral reactions. Yet every time, his throat would close up, his mind would go blank, and his body would tense all over. He was doing it now, even though they were far away from the launch site and still a few days away from lift-off.

"Take charge of yourself, Oleg! You cannot afford this folly," he lectured himself silently.

If Laika disappeared, he'd be forced to use Albina, unless, of course, she disappeared as well. But if that happened, he knew without a doubt what would come next. With two dogs gone, he would not escape suspicion and scrutiny. No doubt the doctor himself, the very important Oleg Gazenko, would ultimately vanish from the photos he'd hidden in his desk drawer, from news reports, from all of history.

He shivered in the cold, started the car again, turned it around and sped back toward Moscow.

8.

The walls in their apartment were so thin that Lilia and Galina had to pad about like kittens as they stuffed themselves into warm sweaters and long skirts over their winter underwear. Lilia packed whatever food she could find in a cloth sack; paper would make too much noise. As if she were leaving for work, Galina gathered her purse and camera bag; her press credentials might come in handy. They carried their coats and boots, tiptoeing in sock feet to the back door of the apartment and carefully down the back stairs. Victor's thunderous snoring had covered their tracks so far. Now at the door to the back alley, they sat on the bottom step and cautiously pulled on their boots, then stood, buttoned their coats and wrapped woolen scarves around their heads and throats, bracing themselves for the cold dead of night outside.

Galina looked at Lilia to make sure they were both ready; they'd vowed not to say a word until they were outside. Lilia nodded, a nervous little smile creeping across her face. Galina returned what she hoped was a confident smile herself, though inside she was terrified to be risking everything — her career, perhaps even her life — for this little dog. No, it was more than the dog, she reminded herself, this was for her sister, who'd done the same for her so many times already, and would surely do so again, if necessary.

"I have just enough money to hire a taxi," Galina said once they were on the sidewalk. "I don't know what we'll do after that."

"It will come to us, the next thing to do," Lilia replied with much more certainty than she felt as the sisters trudged through fresh snow toward the Metro station, where they'd be most likely to find a taxi at this time of night.

"Do you know the address?" Lilia asked her sister.

"Of course," Galina answered. "I wrote it down."

"How will we get inside?"

Galina took her sister's arm to hurry her along.

"It will come to us when we get there."

9.

Korinna was uncharacteristically groggy when she awoke a little past midnight. She thought she'd heard noises outside. She shook her head to clear it and brushed her messy hair away from her face with one hand as she used the other to fumble around the quilt she'd been sleeping on, trying to locate her eyeglasses. She had a constant fear of losing her glasses; she was extremely nearsighted, and without them the whole world was so blurry she could not make out faces just a few feet in front of her. Whenever she awoke, there was always a moment of panic, until she had her hands on the glasses and could put them on.

Now the dog cages were soft gray blobs; one seemed to have a white blob inside; the other she could not see. Finally she remembered she'd taken off her glasses before falling asleep and had put them in the pocket of her lab coat. She reached in her hand and found them there, grabbed them and put them on; her heart stopped racing a little, but then there was the noise again, more distinct, as if putting on her glasses had improved her hearing as well. There was someone or something outside the front door. She looked again at the cages, now in focus, and though it was dark, she could make out Albina's little white body, just where she should be, but the other cage — Kudryavka's — was empty!

She jumped up and then froze, trying to make sense of this scene. If Kudryavka was gone, surely Korinna would be blamed for this! She hesitated to disturb the doctor, but knew what she must do. She walked down the hall and knocked on his office door.

"Dr. Gazenko?"

There was no answer. Now a different scenario formed in her sleepy head. He'd lied to her about when they were leaving; he'd taken Kudryavka only and the two of them were already on the plane to the launch site! No, he wouldn't leave Albina behind, would he? He couldn't leave without letting me say goodbye to Kudryavka, could he?

She pushed open his office door. There was the cot where he was supposed to be sleeping. No one was there. Now she thought perhaps he was outside, with Kudryavka — going for a walk after midnight? At least this would explain the strange noises she'd heard. She raced to the front door of the kennel and flung it open to find two kneeling women, one holding a hairpin she'd been using to try and pick the lock.

All three women screamed. The two sisters stood up clumsily in their bulky winter clothes to face Korinna at the door. It was hard to tell which of the three was the most frightened. Korinna found her voice first.

"What are you doing here?" she shouted, looking directly at Galina. "What have you done with the dog? Give her back to me, or I'll call the police!"

"Run!" Galina shouted to Lilia, and the two sisters took off, leaving Korinna mystified, but with no option other than to do what she'd threatened.

"Operator? Please connect me to the police. Yes, this is an emergency."

10.

We were moving in the car again. He'd stopped talking, and I wondered if I'd done something to upset him. I scrunched up next to him on the seat to let him know I was sorry. I even put one paw up across his leg; it is so hard to communicate with humans when no words will come out of your mouth.

Then my ears perked up as I heard the most amazing thing: he was speaking canine! I listened carefully to familiar sounds escaping from his throat: first a soft grunt, followed by a long, deep sigh, and then a series of dog-like whimpers. The meaning was clear: "I am so troubled and I do not know what to do so I can feel better."

I responded with similar sounds, trying my best to comfort him, and we continued our conversation until the movement stopped again, and the next amazing thing happened. He bundled me in the coat I'd been lying on and carried me in his arms from the car to a door I'd never seen before. We were home. Not home, as in the horrid kennel. Not even home, as in my old neighborhood, fading quickly from my memory. This was Gazenko's home; he'd brought me here to live with him!

"Are you awake now?" I heard him ask me, using human words again.

I couldn't answer his question. The events of this night were so far removed from any waking moment I'd ever had, how could I know for sure whether this was a fanciful dream or whether my miserable real life had taken a well-deserved turn for the better?

As he fumbled with one hand in his pocket for a key to let us in, my ears picked up an undeniable sound on the other side of the door: there was another dog inside, not Albina, not any of the kennel dogs — I could tell by sniffing — but a dog I'd never met.

"Laika, I'd like you to meet Smelaya," he said as he pushed open the door. A honey-colored old-lady dog about my size hurled herself toward us.

Could this be true? The dog the others had gossiped about, the one who used to live at the kennel until Gazenko chose her to live with him? He put me down on the floor so the two of us could get acquainted, as he hurried to start up the small heater in the middle of the room. She was older than I'd imagined, I thought to myself as I sniffed her butt thoroughly. She tried to back away from me, but I followed her rear end like a shadow, determined to find out more. She must have been here a very long time; her odor was everywhere. Then a heavenly scent interrupted, and I had to follow it. In the kitchen, Gazenko had set down two bowls full of real dog food! I think I finished mine in one gulp, while Smelaya sat gawking at my poor manners. Then she politely bent toward her own bowl and began eating with tiny, ladylike bites. He laughed at the spectacle and put more food in my bowl.

"Take it easy, Laika," he said. "This is not your last meal." Then there was a catch in his throat and no more words came out. He opened a cabinet, removed some liquid in a bottle and poured himself something clear and pungent to drink, gulping it down quickly. Then we both followed him into the bedroom, Smelaya and I, where she stepped carefully onto a soft little cushion on the floor beside the bed and proceeded to turn around and around until she decided it was time to lie down. Gazenko was sitting on his bed; he'd pulled off his shoes and his sock feet were on the floor next to me. I heard him pick something up from the table next to him and turn a noisy crank over and over, while I tried to wait patiently. I wasn't sure what I was supposed to do next; there was only one cushion and Smelaya had made herself comfortable there.

"Come on, jump up here," he patted the bed beside him and encouraged me to join him, so I did. At first I had to walk around, exploring the corners, sniffing the quilt, pushing my nose into the pillows, until finally he pulled me over to him.

"We need to get some sleep," he told me, climbing under the covers. "Tomorrow is going to be a big day for us."

How could tomorrow possibly top today, I wondered, settling down next to him, my head propped on his chest. He surrounded me with one arm and pulled me closer to his face, kissing my forehead. He lifted the quilt to make room for me and I crawled under the covers with him. We were so close now I could hear his heartbeat next to my skin. I was warm, cozy, secure, and, I realized, happier than I'd ever been in my short little life. I was out of prison, my tummy was full, and I was lying beside the one I'd fallen crazy in love with, while the old lady dog had to sleep on a silly cushion down below. He'd chosen me among all the others; no other human or animal had ever made me feel so special, so valued and adored. I felt a self-satisfied glow creeping into every part of my body. Every muscle and nerve inside me relaxed into the wash of pleasure rolling through me.

Now, of course, I wish I'd stayed awake to savor this moment, but I had no way of knowing things would change again so soon. Besides, it's easy to fall asleep when you have everything you've ever wanted — and more — so that's exactly what I did.

11.

A fist pounding on the door of his shop downstairs finally roused Victor from a sound sleep. He raised himself up and looked at the clock by his bedside; it was 2 a.m. He noticed that his wife's side of the bed was empty. She and her sister must be sitting up all night gossiping again, he groaned to himself. But there was the pounding downstairs again. Victor got up and took a few steps over to the window, opened it and looked out onto the street below.

"Who's there?" he shouted gruffly. "I'm trying to sleep up here!"

"I'm truly sorry to disturb you, sir."

A tall man in a long overcoat and thick *ushanka* stepped back from the awning over the bakery door, into the snow-covered street, and looked up at Victor leaning out the window. Victor squinted into the darkness and recognized his neighbor, the barrister.

"Is there trouble?" Victor's irritation over being awakened was replaced by growing dread. It's only trouble that comes to your door in the middle of the night.

"I'm afraid so. Could you come downstairs and let me in? I need to talk to you."

Victor closed the window and put his overcoat on top of his nightshirt. He walked through the kitchen and peeked into the living room. Neither his wife nor sister-in-law was there. Now he moved more quickly down the stairs and to the bakery door; something must have happened to Lilia and Galina.

"My wife has disappeared!" Victor exclaimed to the barrister as he opened the door and waved him inside. He hurried to turn on lights, then pulled a chair out for his guest and another one for himself.

"Yes, I know. That's why I'm here."

"And her sister, too. Where have they gone?"

"There has been a..." the barrister fumbled for the best word, "...an occurrence this evening, at the Institute of Aviation and Space Medicine, just outside of town."

"What kind of occurrence? And what does this have to do with my wife?" Victor was quite agitated. He stood and began arranging items on the bakery counter, items he'd left in perfect positions when he'd closed the shop this afternoon.

"She and her sister were seen there," the barrister tried to explain, but Victor cut him off.

"She must come home immediately," he shouted. "She has no business at this...Institute." He shook his head in disbelief, then hurried to the door and looked outside, as if willing Lilia to appear in front of him.

"I was hoping you might know where to find her right now," the barrister continued evenly.

"At this Institute, just like you said!"

The barrister remained calm as Victor's agitation increased.

"I'm afraid she and her sister are no longer there. They were observed there earlier, but now they have gone."

Victor held his head in his hands; his brain was beginning to ache with all he was trying to think of at once. He had to find Lilia; that was the first thing. He forced everything else from his mind and headed toward the back stairs.

"I'm going upstairs to put on my trousers and boots. Then I will go and find her, bring her home."

"I can help you search for her," the barrister offered. "It may be best for you to stay here, in case she needs your help when she returns. If you'll tell me where to go, I'll look for her. I have a car."

"She must be found!" Victor was focused on Lilia's safe return. He had not yet considered why his wife and her sister had gone to this Institute in the middle of the night, or why the barrister had come to his bakery, already knowing this news. If he had thought more, he might have been less enthusiastic about enlisting the barrister's assistance.

"Yes, I'll make a list of everywhere she goes. You'll find her and bring her home. I will wait. I can make tea."

He poured water into a pot and lit a burner under it. He grabbed the pencil the barrister offered him and wrote on a paper napkin all the places he could think of that he'd ever heard Lilia and Galina speak of — shopping districts, movie theaters and concert halls, the Metro route he knew his sister-in-law took to work. The teapot screamed for his attention as he finished his list and handed it over to the barrister. He scrambled beneath the counter for cups, saucers and the tin of tea he kept there.

"Perhaps also a list of anyone your wife and sister-in-law know? Friends who might know how to find them?"

Victor grabbed another napkin, his pencil poised above it, but no names came to mind. Galina, he supposed, might socialize with her TASS co-workers, but he didn't know any of their names. Besides her sister and himself, Lilia had no friends. He was suddenly embarrassed for his wife — no friends to speak of! He was determined not to hand the barrister a blank napkin, so he continued thinking, sipping hot tea, hoping to rouse his still-sleepy memory. At last, he scribbled a few words and passed the napkin to the barrister.

"A priest?" The barrister seemed quite surprised.

"At the church around the corner," Victor gestured.

"Ah, yes," the barrister said, as if suddenly remembering. "Thank you, sir. I'm sure this information will bring your wife home to you very soon now."

He left without another word, and without having the cup of tea Victor had prepared for him.

12.

Korinna heard cars approaching and hurried to the front door. She thought she'd called the civilian police, but these shadowy figures getting out of the cars and walking toward her wore no uniforms, only dark over-coats and furry *ushanka*s on their heads. Already rattled by earlier events, Korinna froze at the sight. Was this KGB? Who had sent the KGB? Then she saw another man approaching, someone she recognized, Dr. Yazdovskiy, the Institute director, who rarely visited the kennel, but here he was at such an improbable time, which led Korinna to envision yet another scenario: something dreadful had happened to her boss, Dr. Gazenko, and perhaps also to Kudryavka, and he was here to break the news to her. She rushed into his arms as he entered the kennel door.

"What has happened to Dr. Gazenko?" she wailed. This night had not been kind to her nerves, now as frazzled as her uncombed hair and rumpled lab coat.

Dr. Yazdovskiy separated himself from her. Like most men, he was no fan of female emotion, especially when he had business to conduct.

"I'm asking you the same question," he replied. "Where is Gazenko and where is the dog?"

Korinna sat in a chair, unbelieving as the men in overcoats approached and surrounded her.

"I don't know," she replied.

"And why are you here in the middle of the night?" Dr. Yazdovskiy continued his interrogation.

"I was watching over the dogs while they slept," she explained.

"Exactly," Yazdovskiy replied, pausing to let the implications of his next statement sink in. "And now one of them is missing. Isn't that right?"

"But that lady photographer was here tonight," Korinna protested. "She was trying to break in. She wanted to steal the dog. You should be asking her these questions."

"We will ask the questions to whomever we decide should be asked," she heard one of the dark men standing behind her speak. "Now we are asking you. The dog, which, as you know, is property of the Soviet Union, has disappeared, and you were the last one to see her. Isn't that correct?"

"I suppose so," Korinna had to admit.

"Then," another dark man behind her asked, "what have you done with the dog?"

"I don't know," Korinna slumped in her seat, holding her head and sobbing.

13.

"What did she mean, 'What have you done with the dog?'" Lilia asked her sister, breathlessly, once they had stopped running. They were making their way through the outskirts of Moscow, keeping off the main roads and clinging to the scant neighborhood shadows. This district had sprouted blocks and blocks of new housing construction, much of it still in progress, evidenced by the sleeping bulldozers, cement mixers, piles of lumber and other construction materials. There were no trees anywhere and the streets had yet to be paved, so they stepped slowly and carefully though the snow-covered mud, using downtown lights in the distance to plot their route.

"Perhaps we are too late to save her," Galina mused. "Perhaps Oleg and Kudryavka have already gone to the launch site."

"Wouldn't that girl have known it, if they had?" Lilia struggled to make sense of her sister's reasoning. "You said she takes care of the dogs there."

"You certainly would think so."

"Where's the launch site? Can we go there?"

"It's a secret location. I only know it's far away."

"How far?" Lilia persisted, and suddenly Galina broke out laughing. "This isn't funny," Lilia pouted. "How far?"

"I was just thinking," Galina said between laughs, "that you are asking the questions now. I am usually the one who asks all the questions."

"How else," Lilia said glumly, "will I find out what I need to know?"

14.
October 30

That little bedside machine, the one Gazenko had been playing with before we went to sleep, had kept a quiet rhythm going all night, but now it suddenly started clanging, a most shrill and painful noise, and we were instantly awake. He leaned over, pushed a button on the machine, and it stopped its squawking. For a moment, all was peaceful again, and I settled back down to sleep some more. It was far too soon to wake up again, but he was gently shaking me.

"Wake up, Laika. We have to go to work," he said solemnly.

Then there was Smelaya's face, peeking up onto the bed. She was pawing at him, quite coquettishly for an old lady, I thought. I sat up and stared down my nose at her. Didn't she understand I was the special pet now?

"Just a moment, Smelaya," he told her, standing and pulling on his trousers.

He was in a hurry as he turned back to me, so rushed that he did not take care to disguise his thoughts, and I saw what he'd been hiding behind his eyes. Instinctively I sniffed the air for validation, and there it was, a subtle little scent coming from him that said things were about to change again, and not for the better. This overnight adventure had been a brief deviation from routine, not a new way of life: I had not become his special pet. It was the morning after and we were going back to the kennel. Soon I'd be back in my tiny cage and Smelaya would continue her reign as queen of this house. If Albina were not so polite, she'd sniff me and say to me a little while from now, "I told you so."

I watched Gazenko critically as he sat on the side of the bed, his back to me, putting on his shoes and tying his shoelaces, then rising to tuck his shirt into his trousers and buckle his belt. I kept hoping for another sign, another scent that would tell me I'd been mistaken, but instead he dealt another blow.

"Come, Kudryavka," he called as he left the room, Smelaya bounding behind him. He was back to formalities: no pet names, no sweet talk.

I stayed put, burrowing underneath the bedclothes, drowning in despair. At once I felt both feverish and cold. I sensed all my happy thoughts unraveling and my little heart breaking into pieces; soon I'd be so scattered, I'd never be able to pull myself back together.

"Come now, Kudryavka," he called me again, a mounting urgency in his voice.

I stuck my nose out from underneath the covers and confirmed the smell of breakfast being served, so I jumped down from the bed and followed him, but refused to eat the dog food he'd spooned into last night's bowl. Instead, I sat sullenly watching Smelaya enjoy hers, one tiny morsel at a time. It was excruciating. By now Gazenko was fully dressed and had combed his hair away from his face. He put on his overcoat, picked me up and carried me outside to his car, saying goodbye to Smelaya, who whined and pleaded with him not to leave her all alone. Just before he closed the door, I issued one short bark, telling her to shut up; he'd come home to her this evening, as he did every evening, while I'd remain caged in the kennel. Then I hid my face in the crook of his arm; I couldn't bear to look at him.

As he warmed up the car, I turned my back and sat shivering on the front seat, trying to control my runaway sorrow. I was crushed; I'd been duped into thinking I was the special pet and that it would last forever. Where'd I ever get such a foolish notion?

Then I remembered the one thing I could do that would help me survive. I'd taught myself to do it on the streets whenever tragedy had overcome me, like the time I got separated from my mother, forever, as it turned out, or the time all my babies were born dead.

I could make myself disappear.

I closed my eyes, breathed in and concentrated on this task until I felt calm. I sat quietly on the front seat as he drove, working hard inside to collect and redirect my shattered thoughts. I used each moment that might have renewed my pain as a reminder instead to renew my determination to disguise the pain so that he would never know how much he'd hurt me. Once I'd gained control of my inner self, it was a simple trick to draw the curtains by unfocusing my eyes so they looked at nothing in particular; now he wouldn't be able to see me at all. It would be as if I were no longer sitting here in his car, as if the dog sitting in my place had become some other dog. I knew one thing for certain: I was not his little Laika anymore.

If someone treats you badly, you can complain vigorously or you can keep quiet and pretend it doesn't matter. My chosen course of action — to vanish from his radar — seemed not only prudent at the time, but also necessary. He must have taken my silence for acquiescence, I later reasoned, and I thought perhaps I should have chosen the more demonstrative option. If I'd just acted on all that was inside me, if I'd sat there on his bed, refusing to vacate the new territory I'd claimed overnight, or if I'd let him know everything I was feeling as we drove back to the kennel, maybe I'd have survived a little longer.

But maybe not. Gazenko had, as some Americans were fond of saying, "screwed the pooch," and that screwed pooch was me. We Russians called it "*vlapils'a*," finding yourself in a really bad situation without any way out. Once you've put your paw into something so deep, I think things can only get worse, until they turn so absolutely hopeless that even the person responsible for the stinking deed has no way of fixing things up; the best he can do is get away from it himself.

He must have sensed my transformation. All the way back to the kennel, he said nothing. By the time we arrived and he carried me from the car, I'd achieved my goal. I'd rewritten our history. I was in the arms of a stranger, and last night had never happened.

"Good girl," he scratched my head as we approached the kennel door. His touch was gentle, yet void of emotion, as if his own thoughts were far, far removed from this time, this place, as if I were some stray dog he'd just grabbed from a Moscow street and dumped into a cardboard box, as if the last few weeks had never happened.

15.

Now that the sun was up, the sisters knew they needed a new plan.

"We didn't do anything wrong," Galina reasoned out loud. "So I'll go to work as usual, and you'll go home. Slip up the back stairs and I'll be home early to help you explain things to Victor. Don't worry; we'll make it my fault that you left the house last night."

"No explaining." Lilia resisted. "He'll not care about any explanation. He'll just be in a fit of anger. Please, no, I can't go home."

Galina knew her sister was right. She couldn't send Lilia home alone to face the certainty of Victor's wrath. Lilia wouldn't be safe there, but where?

"I know," Lilia suddenly brightened. "I can go to the church."

"Are you insane? This is not a time for worshiping."

"No, but the priest will take me in. I can stay with him until you can come home. By then we'll have another plan, yes?"

"Yes, it will surely come to us," Galina promised her sister. She would ask today about her new apartment.

Maybe it would be ready soon and she could take her sister to live there, just the two of them, like before Victor came along. Maybe they'd move into a nice new neighborhood like the ones they'd just walked though as the sun rose. Maybe their new apartment would have big windows to catch the warmth of the morning sun, and window boxes to hold red geraniums in the summer.

"In the meantime, I will pray for us," Lilia promised, as if reading her sister's mind. "Since that's really all I can do."

"Okay, you do that," Galina said without much conviction. Praying all day long was not much of a plan, but if her sister wanted to do this, what could it hurt? There was a Metro stop just ahead. Galina got on a train heading in one direction, toward TASS, and Lilia boarded a train heading the opposite way, back toward their neighborhood. They waved at each other from the train windows, as if this were any other day and they were saying goodbye in that superficial way everyone does when there is no thought of not seeing each other again at the end of the day.

16.

Oleg saw immediately that he'd walked into a scene of barely contained chaos. There were chairs and tables overturned, signs askew, and papers scattered about as if a cyclone had hit. In the center of it all sat poor Korinna, sniffling and wiping her tears and runny nose on the sleeve of her smock. Several strange men stood silently behind her, and his boss, Dr. Yazdovskiy, eyed him reproachfully.

Without commenting, Gazenko hurried down the hall to check on Albina and to return Kudryavka to her cage.

"A word," he heard his boss standing behind him, and the two men went into Gazenko's office and closed the door. Yazdovskiy emerged a short while later.

"There has been a misunderstanding," he explained to the dark-coated men. "The dogs are safe. My chief doctor saw a need to remove the one called Kudryavka from the kennel for some last-minute training. The preparation of the dogs is at his full discretion, you know."

Then he began giving orders.

"You," he said to the men, "put this place back in order before you leave. And you," he said, directing his attention to Korinna, "go home now."

The men in dark coats were not so menacing as they went about their assigned work, righting tables and chairs, gathering paperwork into neat stacks, setting a desk lamp in its proper position. Korinna thought for a moment that she would ask to stay, but her frayed emotions told her she could not take much more; she went to find her coat and purse.

"Dr. Gazenko and I thank you for taking care of the dogs," Dr. Yazdovskiy told her as she left for home, as if this were the end of any other workday. Dr. Gazenko was nowhere to be seen, in his office "catching up on paperwork," his boss had explained.

Once the men in dark coats had departed, Yazdovskiy locked the front door of the kennel and burst angrily into Gazenko's office. Oleg was lying on his back on the cot, one arm covering his eyes against the early morning light beaming through the window.

"Gazenko, you worthless tramp of a man!" his boss railed against him. "There is one reason and one reason only I have not turned you in to the KGB."

"Yes, I know that, sir. Thank you for not doing that."

"Don't thank me. Thank your lucky stars that today above all other days, the space program demands your expertise. The dogs respond to you as to no one else."

"Of course, I will do whatever is asked of me." He sat up slowly and dangled his long legs, little-boy-like, over the side of the cot. "I'm ready, sir."

"Then get the dogs ready now," Yazdovskiy ordered him. "We must leave within the hour."

17.

The neighborhood priest was having a very bad day. Even though he'd been praying non-stop for divine intervention, the Lord had not yet answered his prayers, and the evil men in dark coats would not go away.

They'd knocked on his door just after dawn this morning, awakening him, then shoving him back inside and out of their way as soon as he opened his door a crack.

"Are you hiding someone here?" one had asked him, and when he'd answered, "No, I'm not," another one said they did not believe him — and him a priest! They'd searched his room, tossing his meager possessions this way and that; one, who declared himself in charge, grabbed the priest's cowboy hat from its hook by the door and tried it on. Wearing the hat and a devilish grin, this man sat watching the priest, who crouched in a corner, while the others searched the church sanctuary, surprising and removing some early morning worshippers who'd come to light candles and say prayers.

The priest knew there was nothing he could do to defend himself. He was a man of God, and religion was not easily tolerated under the Communist government. Yet since Stalin's death, there seemed to be less objection to it. There were churches everywhere; what was Khrushchev going to do, tear them all down? And many citizens still worshipped, though he had to admit, more in secret than openly. Their limited attendance to everyday mass meant limited offerings, one reason he lived in such poverty, but he knew his parishioners should not be blamed for their secular fears.

He'd offered the man in charge some tea, hoping to make some for himself in the process; this was a cold morning and he did not have coal to burn in his little heater. The man said he had not come for tea; he'd come for information.

"What is it you need to know?"

"Did a woman named Lilia come here and discuss her concerns about the dog Kudryavka?"

The priest could not lie, yet he'd never known the woman as anything except the baker's wife, nor the stray dog who'd disappeared by any name at all. There was little doubt in his mind now that this was the dog who'd barked on the radio, the one who would be flying soon into outer space. Otherwise, why would this man care?

"Neither name is familiar to me," he answered truthfully, thanking the Lord and praying diligently for another question he could answer honestly without implicating himself or the baker's wife. Lilia, the man in charge had called her. It was a beautiful name.

The interrogation was suddenly interrupted by a soft knock on the front door.

"Who's there?" the priest was ordered to call out.

"It's me," a woman's voice had answered. "It's cold out and I was hoping we could have some tea."

"Giddyap, cowboy," the man wearing the tall black hat chuckled and pushed the priest toward the door. "I think your girlfriend just rode into town."

18.

The KGB was waiting when Galina arrived at TASS headquarters. No one would speak to her or look her in the eye; the secret police moved in and surrounded her, herded her down the hall into her boss's office, and pushed her into a chair. Her boss sat at his desk, calmly watching.

"I've done nothing wrong," she protested. "Why are you doing this to me?"

"Now you will see," her boss said to her, "that these gentlemen can ask even more questions that you can."

One of the men held a photo in front of her face, the one with Gazenko and Kudryavka.

"Did you take this photograph?"

"Yes, of course I did. It's my job to take photographs. He assigned me to do this." She pointed at her boss, still seated behind his desk.

"And you also know that the dog in this picture has been chosen as the space dog?"

"She knew," her boss answered for her. "She told me this, even before the radio announcement. That's why we had the pictures ready to send across the wires."

"You told me to print the pictures, just in case," Galina defended herself. "Why will you not defend me to these people?"

Looks were exchanged among all the men present, and Galina realized it was her boss who had implicated her. He had turned her in to the KGB; now he shuffled papers on his desk, rather than look her in the eye and answer her question.

"You must come with us now," one of the men told her.

"I'll do nothing of the sort," she told him. "I told you I've done nothing wrong."

"You were seen at Gazenko's kennel," her boss said with a tired sigh. "An eyewitness has identified you there."

"Then someone should talk to Dr. Gazenko," she protested. "He will tell you I'm welcome there at any time. Go ahead; ask him!"

"We cannot ask him," one of the men told her. "He has left the kennel. His whereabouts are unknown."

Another man grabbed her by the arm, stood her up and marched her down the hall toward the front door, while everyone she'd known and worked with turned away as she passed. She was put in the back seat of a big black car, and the car drove quickly away.

Inside the news bureau, employees were shaken. One of their own had been arrested. Already rumors circulated that Galina would be charged with subversive activity; most likely she'd end up in a gulag. Each one of them mentally reviewed everything he or she had said, done, written or photographed recently, hoping not to suffer a similar fate.

"Back to work now," Galina's boss emerged from his office.

The news bureau, the official voice of the Soviet government, had just received word that the dog was *en route* to the launch site. The launch of Sputnik 2, with its canine passenger, was imminent. More pictures of the soon-to-be-famous space dog would be needed; these would be sent out by Galina's boss — without Galina's photo credit. Already she had vanished from the news bureau. If anyone had asked, that person would have been told a photographer named Galina had never worked there.

19.

On the big, turbo-prop airplane now flying toward the Cosmodrome, there were seats for fifty passengers, but only six were occupied, three of these by canines in cages. At the last minute, the Institute director, Dr. Yazdovskiy, had decided to bring another doctor, in addition to Gazenko, whom he was no longer sure he could trust, and a third dog, Mushka, in addition to Kudryavka and Albina, chosen from the others randomly, just in case a last minute stand-in was required. At the very least, they could use the third dog for necessary ground testing prior to the launch, saving the space dog and her backup from extra stress or fatigue.

"I'm reminded of an interesting story about when I first came to work for the Institute," Dr. Yazdovskiy told the third doctor, seated next to him. "When they told me I'd be working on preparations for manned space flight, I asked them to show me what had been done so far. They handed me one sheet of paper, and on the paper was a sketch of a dog, more of a doodle than a useful illustration. It looks as if I'll have to start from scratch, I told them. Dog, scratch — get it?"

The third doctor, an underling, laughed appropriately at Yazdovskiy's anecdote.

"That's a good one," the third doctor agreed, pointing to the dogs sleeping in cages across the aisle. "And yet, so very prescient...."

Oleg sat apart from the others, staring vacantly out the airplane window as they flew over familiar patterns of roads networking small villages and neatly plowed farmland that gradually gave way to the bleak monotony of the steppes. Like the other two men, he'd dressed in his official military uniform before boarding the airplane, and now he was thinking that it was only his uniform that made him acceptable to his country and to this space mission. Inside he was nothing but incompetence and failure. His personal weaknesses had nearly ruined them all. Most of all, he was ashamed of himself for not taking better care of Laika in her final days. What he'd done last evening, removing her from the kennel and taking her home with him, was for his own pleasure, not hers. He'd been hoping to assuage his own inner turmoil and guilt over what was about to happen, but instead he'd made things worse for them both.

He'd wanted somehow to explain it all to her, the way he'd often explained it to himself.

You see, Laika, all of life is a test, but some parts of the test are harsher than others. There are places even on Earth in which survival is difficult — locations like deserts with unbearable heat and winds, mountaintops with frigid temperatures and limited oxygen, or deep in the ocean, where there is too much pressure and no oxygen at all. But how can we ever know what is survivable until such extremes are tested? In every challenging situation, there exists a divide between life and death, but the exact location of that boundary cannot be established unless some brave soul approaches, and then crosses it. If that individual crosses and is still alive, then we have established that living souls can bear that much more, and we plan another test for a more distant boundary.

That is why you have become so special to me, to all of us here at the Institute. You will be the first living, breathing creature to test the boundaries of survival in outer space. As such, you are critical to the future success of the Soviet space program, which will soon send men and women into orbit and beyond. But you will become so much more than that, dear Laika. You and your journey to places no one has ever ventured will not only provide us with more knowledge on how to equip ourselves for future trips into outer space; you and your mission will also create an inspiring symbol of Soviet strength, courage and resolve. Soon you will become the most famous and revered dog in the world.

When he'd thought all these things earlier in the mission, and had even written them down in the journal he kept in his desk drawer, he had not considered the fact that the chosen dog may not want to achieve such space heroics. She may want instead what most dogs want: love, affection and a secure place as a special pet in someone's home.

This is what his impulsive and highly inappropriate adventure last night had taught Gazenko at last: Laika only wanted what he'd provided Smelaya years ago, and she looked to him as the only one who could give it to her. Instead, he'd demonstrated to her exactly what she could never have and he now realized this was the greatest disservice he could have done to the little dog. He'd dangled lifelong happiness in front of her face, then snatched it away forever, and soon she would be dead. He'd failed his Laika, and there would be no way to make it up to her. Time was too short and the stakes were too high.

20.

I had to admit I was happy to see Albina again; she was always so sure of herself, and she seemed to understand exactly what was happening to us now.

"This is the way it begins," she'd explained to me, as we were carried out of the kennel in our tiny cages by two men we didn't know, and placed in the back seat of a big black car.

Neither of us, however, could understand why Mushka had been invited to come along on our adventure. She had learned very little at the kennel; she'd seemed only interested in having fun. Whenever we were let out into the kennel yard for exercise, she'd run herself silly; then she'd roll in the dirt, sometimes knocking over our water supply and creating a messy mud bath for herself and others who dared follow her example. Finally she'd collapse in near exhaustion, tongue dangling from her open mouth. This dog Mushka had no self-control at all, and was definitely not of the same caliber as Albina and myself. It was almost as if they'd grabbed the least-prepared dog at the last minute. It was an insult to our superb accomplishments, I whined to Albina.

Even so, Albina said, we must be nice to her. I said I'd consider this, but the matter was far from settled, in my opinion.

"So what happens next?" I asked the expert.

"We will get in a bigger car," she'd answered, "but this car will not only go forward; it will also go up. And it will move very fast."

"It will fly?" I'd never been off the ground before, and had to admit the prospect was intriguing. "How does it feel to fly?"

"It's scary at first, especially in your stomach, but you get used to it."

That's where we were now, flying with Mushka and the three men in an enormous and noisy car that had risen into the sky. Albina had been right, of course; my stomach had turned over several times when we began. I could tell we were going higher and faster, but still this was nothing compared to the torture room back at the kennel. After a while, I couldn't even tell we were moving. When I noticed the other two dogs were napping, I decided to do that, too, confident that when we all woke up, Albina would explain what would happen next.

Imagine my surprise a little later, to hear Albina hissing at me.

"Where were you?" she wanted to know.

I didn't want to answer, at least not truthfully, so I pretended not to hear.

"Last night," she persisted, "you left with Gazenko. Everybody knew."

I'd never seen Albina behave like this before. She must be jealous, I realized with a small upsurge of pride that I'd managed to undo her usual cheery disposition.

"Who told on me?"

"Poodle Girl got all upset when she found the two of you were missing and then things got really out of control. More humans came. They made lots of noise. That's when I finally woke up."

The car we were traveling in dipped sharply down and then back up again; Albina vomited, and I hurried to make amends.

"I didn't mean to upset you," I said, but she'd turned her back to clean herself, and as soon as our car began moving evenly again, one of the humans we didn't know got up to clean her cage.

21.

It was early afternoon, and Victor realized he'd made a big mistake. He should not have allowed the barrister to go looking for Lilia. He should have done this himself. Hours had passed and he'd heard nothing. He could not concentrate on baking and so he'd retreated upstairs without opening his shop. Several times he'd left the apartment to knock on the barrister's door, but there was no answer. He was becoming frantic, thinking about all the things that might have happened to his wife. Moscow was a dangerous city; that's why he'd tried so hard to keep her safely at home.

Now that he'd had time to think things over, he tried to assemble the few pieces of information he had. Lilia and her sister had left the apartment sometime last evening, after he'd gone to sleep; that was the only thing he could be sure of. Whether or not they had gone to this Institute, as the barrister had reported, he could not know for sure. There was no reason for Lilia to go to such a place, though it was certainly possible her reckless sister may have talked her into some unreasonable adventure. What had the barrister called the place...the Institute of Aviation and Space Medicine. This name meant nothing to him.

The barrister had asked Victor for a list of places and another list of names, which, in his initial panic, the baker had provided without questioning why. Now he wondered whether the barrister was actually looking for his wife and sister-in-law. Perhaps there was another reason he'd required this information.

There was one way to find out, Victor thought as he hurried to pull on his boots, jacket and hat. He'd listed the neighborhood priest as someone Lilia knew. Victor could ask the priest whether the barrister had been by, looking for Lilia. Then at least the baker would know whether the barrister was out searching for Lilia, and he'd know whether this tall, dignified, but secretive man could in fact be trusted.

Victor hurried down the back stairs and out into the street. When he reached the priest's living quarters, he knocked and knocked again, but no one came to the door. Victor went around the corner to the front door of the church and stopped. An avowed atheist, he had not entered a church door since childhood, and yet he wondered, now that he was here, whether he should enter, kneel and pray for his wife's safe return. As he stepped back from the entrance to reason his way toward a decision, one big wooden door creaked open, and a middle-aged woman he'd seen many times in the neighborhood, and sometimes in his bakery, emerged. She blinked in the sunlight and fixed her eyes on him.

"You," she said incredulously, "are here for confession?"

Victor forced a smile as he hurried past her into the sanctuary. Just inside, he removed his hat and stopped again. He'd forgotten religion altogether, and now stood in awe of its trappings, always so elegant, even in austere times. The gilded full-length mirror in the vestibule, the rack of candles lit by parishioners earlier this morning, the wide red-carpeted aisles and polished wooden pews, and finally, the resplendent white-and-gold altar at the front, with its larger-than-life crucifix. Victor inched uncomfortably down a side aisle toward the confessional booth. This, he reasoned, is where I will find the priest. He sat in a pew and watched impatiently until he saw the confessional door slide open; an elderly woman with a white lace headpiece perched crazily on her gray hair exited the booth. It was his turn to approach the confessional. He entered and slid the door closed.

"Father, please, I ask forgiveness for sins I have committed," he whispered with great uncertainty as he knelt before the screen panel that separated him from the priest. Not sure what he should say next, he remained silent.

"How long since your last confession?" he was soon prompted.

"I don't know. It's been a while."

There was another long pause before the next prompt.

"You may confess your sins now."

"All of them?"

"You can begin with the most egregious of these sins."

Victor felt a sudden urge to pull that damned partition off, to trade places with the priest and then make him confess to everything he knew about Lilia's disappearance, but there were other parishioners scattered about. He would have to go through this confession, and perhaps coax some information from the unseen priest along the way. He took a deep breath.

"I have sinned against my beloved wife."

"What kind of sin?"

"I love her, but I have not always been kind to her."

"Can you be more specific about this sin?"

Confession was supposed to be good for the soul, but it certainly was hard on the priest who had to hear it, especially when the person confessing was not cooperative.

"I did something to hurt her."

The priest decided to try the obvious. "Have you been with another woman?"

"No, Father, I have not. She wanted one thing to happen, but I did another."

There was another long pause.

Victor continued, "She wanted to adopt a little stray dog, but I sold it instead to the scientists for their experiments."

On the other side of the screen, the priest struggled to maintain his priestly demeanor. He wanted badly to emerge from his hiding place, shake the evil man by his collar and demand to know why he'd had his own wife arrested. But he could not. He'd vowed to hear any and all confessions, to help absolve them with prayers and contrition, and then, impossibly, to forget everything he'd heard.

An extremely long pause and Victor began to wonder if the priest was still there, but eventually the voice on the other side of the screen spoke again, trembling slightly.

"Do you not think this was also a sin against the little dog?"

"I suppose it might have been," Victor reasoned out loud. "Can I be forgiven for this, Father?"

"Are you truly sorry for what you did?"

"To my wife or to the dog?"

The priest was momentarily taken aback, but knew he must come up with an appropriate answer. He cleared his throat to buy time, finally remembering a conversation he'd had with Lilia.

"St. Francis would say you should love the little dog as much as you love your own wife."

"I'm no saint, Father, but I do love my wife." The awkward intimacy of the confessional suddenly closed in on Victor, and he quietly fled his side of the booth.

He missed the priest's unorthodox dismissal, mumbled toward the ceiling of the confessional: "Who among us *is* a saint? Who among us even comes close?"

22.

I am two men, if not more, the priest lamented to himself as he hurried along the sidewalk later that day, his thin legs weak with fear and nearly buckling underneath his robe as he walked.

The locked bakery door displayed a hastily penned sign: "Sorry, We Are Closed."

If only priests were allowed to post such signs! He knocked on the bakery door, waited, then knocked again.

He had come to tell the baker what had happened earlier this morning. If only the man had not come to confession. Now that he knew it was the baker who'd caused it all, it would be much more difficult to face him, man to man. He prayed for wisdom and for tolerance. The baker should know what had happened to his wife, to Lilia. He realized he did not know the baker's name.

Eventually Victor leaned out the second floor window and yelled. "Go away. The bakery is closed today."

"Please, sir, may I come in?"

Upstairs, Victor heard a weak male voice. The speaker was hidden under the red and green awning. "I have news about...Lilia."

Victor bounded down the stairs and hurried to open the door, expecting the barrister at last. Instead, there stood the mangy priest.

"If you had news, why didn't you tell me earlier today?"

"I'm sorry, sir, but I have not seen you today, until just now."

Victor gestured to the priest — who apparently was now pretending *not* to be the priest — to enter his bakery. This made no sense; no wonder Communism had no need for such religion!

"What do you know about my wife? Have you seen her?"

"She came by early this morning."

"Why would she come to you?" Victor could not believe what he was hearing. "Why did she not come to me?"

"I'm sure I don't know."

"Then what did she say?"

"Very little," the priest fumbled for the right words. "You see, the police were there already..."

"The police!"

"And they took her away. They would not let me accompany her."

"Why has this happened?"

Victor was red-faced and shouting now. The priest took a few protective steps backwards.

"They said they were looking for her, but they did not say why." The priest hoped that if he remained calm, then perhaps the baker would calm down, also. Now, of course, the priest understood why Lilia had come to him instead of this explosive, out-of-control hothead husband of hers.

Lilia should not be with such a man, the priest thought. She should be with someone kinder and gentler, someone who would treasure her and take good care of her, someone who would make her afternoon tea. The third man was speaking now, the most human and the most dangerous man, the one he must work and pray harder to silence.

"I think," the priest advised Victor, "that you should go down to Lubyanka Square and try to find Lilia there." Now that he knew her name, he realized he loved saying it. "I'll go with you if you want." Please let me go along, he thought to himself.

"No, I will handle this," Victor still fumed. He wanted no help from anyone. "I'll find my wife and bring her home."

"Then I will pray that you are successful," the priest said as he left the bakery. That was really all he could do. For Lilia, for himself, for them all.

23.

With great precision, the plane carrying the means to the next success of the Soviet space program put itself down on the tiny runway at the Baikonur Cosmodrome. Earlier today, Number 20 had pitched a fit when he found out they were all traveling together.

"What would happen if there were a crash?" he'd yelled. "Our whole mission would be wiped out."

His workers had learned to ride the crests of his tantrums, which were becoming more common as the launch deadline approached; such outbursts were usually brief and followed by a mantle of absolute calm he'd managed to locate and put on himself.

"Back to work now," he'd always say, as a signal to all that the storm had passed.

It was almost dark by the time we were carried in our cages from the airplane into a nearby building. The day had ended quickly; we'd all napped again and then the humans we didn't know had fed us treats. Gazenko had remained listless, pretending to doze, yet I knew he was not asleep; his eyes remained open, staring vacantly out the window like an uninspired tourist. Mushka wanted to know why.

Albina, who was still not speaking to me, explained to Mushka that Gazenko always behaved this way just before sending dogs into the sky.

"But you said we're already flying," Mushka reminded her.

"This is nothing," she predicted. "Wait until we get to the next part. We'll go higher and faster than you could ever imagine."

"Will it feel like the torture room?" Mushka had struck out early in the contest; she could bear neither the shaking nor the noise.

"Yes, but then it's over and something amazing happens."

"What?" Mushka was trembling with excitement.

"Your whole body becomes light, like air," Albina tried to explain. "Your paws no longer touch the floor and your head bobbles around like a silly toy. It only lasts for a moment, but you'll remember it forever. And it becomes so quiet that you can hear yourself breathing."

"Then what?" Mushka wanted to know.

"Somehow," Albina fumbled for the right words here, "you leap from the box you've been riding in and then you float down to the ground. That can take a long time." She continued more confidently. "There are people down below waiting to catch you and bring you back home."

I was still not convinced Albina knew as much as she professed, even though, I had to admit, she'd been right about everything so far.

"Don't worry," she said, wagging her tail. "We'll be back at the kennel soon, and we'll be showered with treats."

"Even me?" Mushka knew that only two dogs would ride higher into the sky, and she knew she was last in line. Like Albina and me, she must be wondering exactly what she was doing here.

Before long, I decided she was here to serve as our class clown. Either that, or she'd been named the new village idiot. As soon as we were inside and they let us out of our cages, she began dashing around the room, teasing us with her antics. Her mindless exuberance was quite contagious, and soon Albina and I joined in the mayhem. There were tables to run under, chairs to jump in and out of, and new humans to entertain. The men who'd been working at the big desks in the room all stopped to watch and laugh. Some even encouraged us, whistling and clapping as we galloped back and forth, rolled on our backs and yipped back at them.

Suddenly the room went quiet. The door had opened and a man had entered, wearing a white coat and carrying a clipboard thick with papers.

"I see that our dogs have arrived," he spoke quietly. "But still we have work to do, do we not?"

The humans returned to their tasks. Some were reading papers on clipboards, adding occasional notes, while others fiddled with lit-up buttons or cranked knobs on machines mounted to the tables in front of them. The solemn man stood watching intently as they worked. I crept out from under a table to get a good look at him. He was tall, even for a human, and broad in the head and shoulders, mastiff-like. His large dark eyes surveyed all the activity in the room, and finally his gaze moved down to the floor. When he looked directly at me, I knew I'd seen these eyes before. This was the human who'd once visited the kennel, the one whose mind and soul were weighted down with sorrow. How could anyone who saw this look bear to disappoint this man any more? I knew instantly it was time to behave myself; so did Albina, and we both lay down on the floor. But there was foolish Mushka, tiptoeing around the perimeter of the room and then stationing herself just behind him.

"Arf!" she barked suddenly, and when he turned to look, she bowed down on her front legs, tail in the air, wagging madly. She had understood nothing here; she was inviting him to play.

"Where's the trainer?" the man erupted. "Get him in here to take care of his dogs. They should be in their cages. Why are they running loose?"

"They were cooped up in cages all day, sir," Gazenko entered the room and hurried to defend us. "They need to release some of their energy, or they will not be able to settle down and sleep tonight."

"Then take them to another room for their exercise," the man snapped back. "I don't want to see these bitches running wild in my control room again!"

Gazenko had now been joined by the other humans who'd come here with us, and they all busied themselves trying to round us up.

"Once you've put your little darlings to bed," the man continued, "I will see you all in my office. There is much we need to discuss."

"But it might be quite late, sir."

"No matter. I will be waiting." The sad-eyed man turned and left the room.

24.
Lubyanka Square, Moscow

There were several buildings at Lubyanka Square, located prominently near the Kremlin in downtown Moscow; one housed the prison, the others held offices plus training and working areas for the secret police. Everyone knew this location, which had been home of the *cheka* since the Bolshevik Revolution. Many had come to the front door of the yellow building during the Stalin years, searching for friends and loved ones who'd been taken in the middle of the night.

It was said by some that so much information entered these buildings, while so very little came out of it, that the doors might as well have been one-way only. There was no end to blood-chilling stories of torturous interrogations held here with prisoners before they were sentenced and shipped off to remote gulags. But the view from each prison cell was amazing, some still managed to joke: from here you could see Siberia.

In addition to the main door, there were numerous, secret ways to enter and leave the Lubyanka Square complex, about which the general public knew nothing. One could enter an underground tunnel a block away, for instance, pass underneath the city streets surrounding

Lubyanka, and then climb a set of stairs into its fortified center.

Victor took the more familiar underground route; there was a Metro stop at Lubyanka Square. He'd forced himself to take the time to make himself presentable, shaving and dressing in his only business suit before leaving the apartment. It was mid-afternoon by the time he emerged from the train station, blinking in the daylight bouncing off patches of the overnight snowfall, now quickly melting in the sun.

He was surprised that the first person he ran into was the barrister, dressed in an elegant suit, standing just inside the front door. Whether this was coincidental or not, Victor now believed his neighbor knew more than he was telling, and his anger returned; he rushed toward the man, who was nearly a foot taller, grabbed one lapel in his fist and pulled the barrister's face down to his level.

"You tell me where my wife is," Victor hissed. "I've come to take her home."

The barrister was unimpressed by Victor's menacing behavior; he knew they were surrounded by unseen KGB hiding in alcoves or underneath the staircase, ready to respond in a moment's notice.

"Take your hands off me," he whispered sternly, "or you will be arrested."

Frightened by the barrister's un-neighborly demeanor, Victor quickly took a step back.

"You must leave here immediately," the barrister smoothed his clothing and continued in a less hostile voice. "I've been waiting here to warn you. They are looking for you, also."

"I've done nothing." Victor stood his ground.

"That may be," the barrister said, now putting a friendly arm around the baker and moving them both toward the exit. "But some say you have been harboring subversive individuals, and if they find you here, they will most likely want to question you about this."

"There's no one subversive in my home," Victor argued, but knew in his heart this may not be true. He knew little of his sister-in-law's life away from the apartment. Of course Galina may be subversive; he only hoped she'd not convinced Lilia to engage with dangerous ideas or to join in illegal activities.

"Would you perhaps have a different opinion, if this would save your wife? Your sister-in-law, perhaps she has fallen in with the wrong crowd? Could that be possible?"

"I suppose so," Victor answered. "Would my saying so bring my Lilia back to me now?"

They were just outside the front door now. The barrister turned to face Victor, taking both the baker's shoulders in his hands and shaking him gently but firmly.

"Please understand that I am trying to save both you and your wife," he whispered urgently. "But this may take some time. So go home now. I will bring you news by the end of the day."

Victor did not want to leave Lubyanka Square without his wife. That, in his mind, would be failure on his part. Yet, he reasoned, if he ended up in jail, how could he ever help Lilia get out of whatever trouble her sister had gotten her into? He looked back at the building from which he and the barrister had just emerged; there were uniformed men now waiting just inside. The decision to stay or go was not his, after all. He turned and descended the stairs to the underground Metro station.

The barrister sighed with relief. He did not need this volatile man bothering him until he'd sorted everything out. If the baker behaved himself now, and if he offered useful information, he might still be spared. The barrister knew already that the baker's wife was doomed; he'd known that from the moment his associates told him they'd found one of her hairpins just outside the kennel at the Institute. While a citizen could certainly be incarcerated based on reports from other citizens acting as witnesses, there was much more value in even the flimsiest piece of hard evidence. A tiny hairpin alone could assure a sentence of ten, maybe twenty years.

Part Four

Commitment

1.
Baikonur Cosmodrome
October 31, 1957

I'm going to say all of this in canine, but if you pay attention, I think you will understand me.

We have been a great disappointment to each other, you and I.

You wanted me to be sweet like Albina, but it's just not my nature to be that nice, and the harder I've tried, the worse it's made me feel. I can't pretend any longer to be something I'm not.

Which brings me to the next point.

We have been fooling each other, you and I.

I put on a grand performance because I wanted you to like me best. I wanted you to choose me from among all dogs as the one you'd most treasure, as the one you'd take home to be your special pet, and in so doing, I forgot I was just pretending.

Meanwhile, your own act was so convincing that when you took me home with you, I believed I'd live with you forever. But when we got there, I realized you'd already chosen Smelaya as your special pet. I knew there was no place for me in your life, and that you'd had another reason for pretending to like me so much.

So, no more pretending, all right?

He'd come for me first thing this morning, gently but wordlessly attaching a leash to my harness, and walking me outside the ugly concrete building where Albina, Mushka and I had slept in our cages last night. The sky was clear and the sun was just edging up over the flat horizon. There was no end to the cold gusts of wind that seemed to blow us in all directions at once, carrying multiple scents of humans and machines, but not any specific smell I could identify. There were no familiar buildings, no trees, no streets full of people and traffic in this desolate place.

I paused now to sniff a small scrub bush, then squatted beside it to pee. When I'd finished, I looked up to see if he was getting any of this. I thought I saw him nod, a good sign, so I continued.

I think the time has passed for trivialities, and no matter what the brilliant Albina says, I think there is a unique fate in store for me. You have chosen me for some reason that I cannot fathom, to do some thing that you must be convinced I can do. Whatever this thing is, I will do it as best I can, so that the trust you have put in me will not be in vain. I am smart and I am strong; I will not disappoint you. Do you understand?

I needed to squat again, this time by what looked like a tall metal waste can. This walk outdoors was my first chance here to mark new territory. So far I'd smelled no other dogs along our route, but now any who showed up would know I'd been here first.

I looked at him again. He seemed stalled, deep in thought; I walked ahead and tugged the leash so he'd follow, determined to say what was on my mind, to address all the unfinished business between us, and to make certain he understood. I'd composed my speech last night, after the others had gone to sleep, and I'd rehearsed it over and over. I may only have this one chance to deliver it.

I see now that this thing between us is not true love, at least not the way I'd envisioned it; but you have to admit there is something like love between us, something that draws me to you, and you to me, something that demands we both acknowledge what we feel.

Another pause, this time by a mound of colorless grass. I was almost done.

It's a feeling that reminds me of another human I once knew, a man with skinny legs who fed me, and was kind to me. But soon he asked for something in return; something I was not willing to give him. I hurt him instead, and think now that was a mistake; I think love, if that is all we have to call it, requires some positive action on both sides, or it cannot be sustained. And what good is this feeling, if it does not last?

Which brings me to my final point.

What I want from you is this: Do not ever forget our time together. Do not ever pass through a whole day and go to bed at night without thinking of me. No matter how far apart we are from each other, no matter how much time passes, I will think of you always, and I ask that you do the same.

Perfect timing; I finished my speech just as our walk concluded. One more convenience stop, this time by a fence post so new I could still smell the tree it came from, and we went back inside. I'd said everything on my mind. I felt unburdened, satisfied, even hopeful, as he handed me over to a young man in a white smock who'd been waiting just inside the door.

"OK, Laika," I thought I heard him whimper quietly as I was carried away from him.

2.

Names mean so much to humans that they spend precious time inventing them, but all that had changed drastically in this place. Gazenko was given a number when he arrived; here he would be referred to as Number 72. The Chief Designer had been known as Number 20 since arriving nearly two weeks ago. There was no logic for which number was assigned to which human, but then there was so much new information here, and very little of it made sense.

The young man who'd taken me from 72 just now, for instance, was called "11." He seemed to have been assigned the tasks that Poodle Girl had performed back at the kennel. That was another odd thing; except for us dogs, there were no females here, which changed the overall scent of the place dramatically. I'd enjoyed Poodle Girl's smells during her careful ministrations to me, the grooming and even the bathing, but I had to admit this Number 11 was just as sweet and gentle as she had been, even though his smell was different, and the odor of the bath was horrific as usual.

"How's that?" he asked as he set me down in a tub of warm soapy water and trickled some of it on my head and back. Human cleanliness is nothing like canine cleanliness; what most humans don't understand is that dogs are perfectly clean without all the fussing about with the washcloth and soapsuds, which to us stink to high heaven.

After my bath, Number 11 sat me on a table and dried me off, then proceeded to bathe me again! This time he poured smelly water from a bottle and used a sponge to wipe me all over; this bath was colder and made me shiver. Two baths in row, when none were needed; this would be an amusing anecdote I could use to entertain Albina next time I saw her. I longed to get back into her good graces. She and Mushka had both been sleeping when I left this morning, but surely they were awake now.

I had not seen any dog or human for several hours, except for Number 11, who by now had dried me again, combed my hair with a fine-toothed comb, and then, inexplicably, had painted small circles on my head, neck and chest, finally covering the circles with smelly white powder. After that, he moved me to another table, where he dressed me in one of the silly outfits they'd made me wear back at the kennel. So silk jackets and trousers are stylish in this place as well. I hoped they'd brought outfits for Albina and Mushka, also. Maybe they'd take our picture when we were all gussied up: three gals dressed to go out on the town, albeit a very strange town, where no one seemed to know how to have fun.

Surely Mushka would be able to convince them otherwise; I was beginning to appreciate her unrestrained giddiness. And by now, I had almost decided that, as soon as I regained her trust, I'd ask sweet Albina to be my very best friend. This was a big deal for me; I'd never had a best friend before, and wasn't exactly sure what all was involved, but I was sure Albina would know exactly what we were supposed to do, and could effortlessly explain it all. I was looking forward to the trip we'd take, and then to more good times back at the kennel, which we'd soon rule together, sharing our precious but well-deserved top dog status as only best friends could, whipping the others into shape, inventing new tricks we could teach the humans, howling to upset Poodle Girl, and eventually figuring out the best way to share our beloved Gazenko.

3.

Number 20 watched the enormous doors of the assembly building slide open. Inside, giant engines rumbled to life and ever so slowly the R-7 missile sleeping horizontally on a customized flatbed rail car was roused and began rolling slowly into the sunshine. This was the only float in the short but critical parade route from the building to the launch pad, and Number 20 and his closest associates walked alongside it as other workers gathered on both sides of the railroad track to observe the slow journey of only 1.5 km, but one that had to be made so carefully that it took the better part of an hour to get there. Then a concentrated burst of human activity inched the missile, bottom first, into its exact position, locked it in place, attached guidelines, checked and re-checked everything as Number 20 looked on. Finally, another groaning engine started the massive elevator designed to lift the missile into its vertical launch position. There was no cheering as it rose, no human noise of any kind. This was the most solemn of occasions. Every mechanical part must work flawlessly; there would be no time to repair anything that malfunctioned, and everyone involved in these last, critical processes knew how much responsibility rested on his shoulders.

Number 20 bore perhaps the greatest possible burden on his own broad shoulders: maintaining the Soviet Union's so-far impressive lead in the global space race, and insuring his own continuing role in the rapidly evolving Soviet space program. It was he who'd shaken Khrushchev's hand just a few weeks ago, guaranteeing the success of Sputnik 2, and it was he who'd suffer most if anything went wrong. He stood stiffly erect at the base of the launch pad, pushing these troubling thoughts from his tired brain, struggling to stay focused in the moment, shielding his eyes in the morning sun and straining his thick neck to see the pointed top of the third stage as it climbed the launch pad. He listened for the sound of the missile being locked into place, then allowed himself to take a deep breath.

Most, but not all, had gone as planned, since final preparations for launch had begun the day before. Just as he'd anticipated, the arrival of the dogs and the doctors had set off a wave of frenzied excitement among the workers that he'd just barely been able to contain. And the great Dr. Gazenko himself apparently had not been on his best behavior just prior to leaving Moscow with the others bound for the Cosmodrome, as his boss Dr. Yazdovskiy, now Number 58, had confided as soon as they'd landed. In the meeting Number 20 had with all the doctors late last night, he'd made it clear that all their activities here were under his own guidance; there would be no independent decisions made. The biological crew was subsumed under the larger space mission umbrella, under the explicit and unquestionable command of The Chief Designer, Number 20.

"You do nothing without my OK," he told them flatly, "and whatever I OK, you do. This is what the mission demands."

After the meeting, he'd sent the doctors to get some sleep, but he did not take the opportunity himself to rest. Instead, he went over his notes, both mental and on stacks of paper, playing each event over and over in his head, trying to visualize any possible glitch, so as to prevent it from happening.

The dog, one of the three running wild last night in his control room, was the least predictable element. Even though both Gazenko and his boss vouched for her exemplary performance in all training tests, Number 20 was still suspicious. He did not like having any females at the launch site, but here was one exception he had to allow.

The uncertain combination of both Gazenko and his dog over the next few days, however, seemed too potentially disruptive. Near dawn, Number 20 made an executive decision; the dog would be sealed into her space cabin today, three days before launch. They would use the time to test and re-test every instrument in her cabin. They would make sure she was eating, breathing and excreting as she should. There were plenty of logical reasons to explain this sudden revision to the pre-announced launch schedule. He did not have to reveal the most important one, the confidential telephone call he'd received yesterday with details about the security breach at the Institute in Moscow, about Gazenko taking the dog for a joyride, and about the mysterious women who'd been caught trying to break into the kennel. One of the women, it was reported, had been to the kennel before, and had befriended Gazenko. Both women had been arrested promptly and a full investigation was underway.

Number 20 did not have time for such human drama, nor could he afford any last-minute crises. His announcement went out over the intercom immediately. Number 72, the doctor who had prepared the dog for this mission and to whom the dog responded as to no one else, was told to take her for a short walk as soon as the sun rose, and then to hand her over to Number 11, the designated groomer, for final preparations.

4.
Lubyanka Prison, Moscow

Lilia could not sit down. She could see nothing in the dark and she could barely breathe. There was no food offered and no place to relieve herself. She'd been locked inside an airless, vertical box, hardly bigger than a coffin, and that's where she'd spent the night, resting her weight on one foot, then the other, all the while crying her eyes out. Every sound she heard created new panic in her frightened and confused mind. There were footsteps, back and forth, often accompanied by muffled voices and clicking tongues. Once she'd heard a woman's voice and thought it might be Galina coming for her, so she called out with as much volume as she could muster:

"I'm here. Please help me, Galina."

But the only response was a hard boot kick on the wall of her tiny closet, sending vibrations throughout her terrified body. The men who had grabbed her as soon as the priest opened his door yesterday would tell her nothing as they stuffed her into the back of a black sedan. She was blindfolded before being moved from the vehicle and walked here to this place. Just before they shut the door, one turned her away and pulled the blindfold from her eyes. Then the door slammed shut and she heard the clicks of their boot heels as they walked away.

More than anything, she wanted to know about her sister, whether an identical fate had befallen Galina, and whether she was somewhere nearby. Even when they were in the worst of all possible situations, having each other to hold onto had always gotten them through it. Being alone, absolutely alone, was new for Lilia. She did not know whether she could survive it.

Galina had heard what she thought was her sister crying as they led her toward her own tiny prison cell, but before she'd even had a chance to cry out, one of the men had clamped his hand over her mouth. She'd bitten him as hard as she could.

That's why she'd ended up here, in another room, being "prepped" for her initial interrogation. She was stripped and every area of her body was searched, her tangled hair pulled painfully as a female guard combed through it with a fine-toothed comb before investigating her ears, mouth and even her private areas with a flashlight. She was held under a cold shower, and afterwards given a thin prison gown to cover her shivering self, and even thinner slippers for her feet.

Finally, her name was taken away and she was given a number: 57706.

"Confess your crimes," the uniformed interrogator who sat behind a desk barked when she'd been seated across from him. A guard stood on either side of her chair and another stood behind her. These were bigger, meaner looking men than the ones who'd met her at the news bureau. The one she'd bitten in the hallway had disappeared.

"I have nothing to confess," she replied, and the guard behind her grabbed a strand of her hair and pulled it hard. All the guards here must be trained in pulling hair, she decided.

The interrogator referred to papers on a clipboard resting in front of him on the desk.

"You are known to have possessed stolen government property. Is this true?"

"I don't know what you're talking about."

"You are lying!"

Another pull on her hair. Galina's head was aching.

"Then why don't you tell me all about it?"

"Shut up! I will ask the questions here!"

But there were no more questions; suddenly the interrogation was over.

"We will talk again soon," the man at the desk warned her as she was led away to one of the little closets and locked inside.

5.
Baikonur Cosmodrome

We were traveling again, this time straight up. Number 11, now joined by two more white-coated men, carried me carefully in his arms into a tiny room with windows all around. Another man closed the door and pushed a button; the whole room started rising slowly. My stomach turned over once and I hid my face in the bend of Number 11's elbow, but just as I was getting used to the feeling, the room stopped moving. I looked around as the door slid open and we stepped out onto some kind of platform in the sky. I could see all around: the route where I'd walked this morning with Gazenko, the ugly gray building where I'd spent the night. I looked hard into the distance, thinking I'd be able to see Moscow from here, maybe even my old neighborhood, but there was only flatness in all directions, nothing I could recognize. The last time I'd seen the sun, it was just appearing on the horizon; now it was nearly straight up overhead.

"Here we go, Kudryavka," Number 11 crooned in my ear as another man opened a tiny box like the one I'd been put in before, back at the kennel. Finally something familiar; I wagged my tail excitedly — I knew this routine! They'd stick the strange little poop bag to my rear and they'd attach my harness to the sides of the box. They'd close the door and leave. All I had to do was wait. Eventually a pellet of food would show up, I'd eat it, and later I'd relieve myself in the poop bag. Then they'd all rush in like Gazenko used to, releasing me from the box and telling me how wonderful I was. There would be treats.

Sure enough, once the box was opened up, on went the poop bag and in I went. This time, the men fussed over me a lot more than usual, attaching wires from the sides of my box to my chest, my head and neck. One wrapped a wide rubber sash around my middle; another hooked a little container to that loose piece of skin on my neck. Two of the men checked and re-checked each attachment, while the third wrote down the results they called out to him, just like Gazenko used to do. As they worked me over, I could smell something new coming from them all, fear mixed with dread, and I wondered, honestly, what there was to be so concerned about. Maybe, since they didn't know me well enough, they were worried that I might not pass this test. Don't worry, I tried to let them know with a short but confident bark. I can ace this one!

Then another unusual thing happened. Just before closing the door of my little box, Number 11 leaned in and kissed me on the nose. The other two men did the same. This was not flirtation, I could tell: more like a solemn farewell. Their work here must be done and they'll be leaving soon, I thought.

"Bon voyage," Number 11 said, words I did not understand, although he seemed sincere in saying them to me. The door was closed tightly, and all three stood for a moment watching me through a round clear window before they walked away.

Nice as they were, these nameless men could never take Gazenko's place, but it turns out I'd remember them also, for their final kindnesses to me.

6.
Lubyanka Prison, Moscow

The neighborhood barrister, whose name was actually
Boris Petrov, had been given a small, windowless room on
the third floor of Lubyanka Prison to use as his office during the investigation; he'd been assigned as a prosecutor
in the sisters' case, a decided step up in his legal career,
and a way to transition from the routine practice of civil
law to a high profile position in the new legal system run
by the Communist Party. Already he'd filled several pages
with his handwritten notes, many copied from previous
notes he'd made during his investigation. As soon as he'd
been told they had arrived, he'd completed the paperwork
necessary to process the sisters — now known as prisoners 57706 and 55905 — stating the formal charges against
each of them.

His written reports would be used by interrogators
to coax confessions from the prisoners. In this prison,
interrogations were short but frequent; in between, the
prisoner was given time to "think things over," then bom-
barded again with "evidence" of a crime committed. Each
time the interrogator would make notes of everything the
prisoner said. Petrov would take these notes after each interrogation session and use them to prepare a fresh, new
written confession, which the prisoner would be shown at
the next session, and asked to sign. No matter how long

it took, nor how many sessions, nor how many confession documents, without proper food or hygiene, eventually all prisoners (but especially the females — who were used to a more comfortable lifestyle with hot water, a change of underwear and a tube of lipstick) would sign the confession, which then would become primary evidence presented at the trial.

In addition to his handwritten notes, Petrov kept a cigar box in the tall, gray filing cabinet they'd moved into his office yesterday. Inside were pieces of evidence he'd collected: Lilia's hairpin found near the kennel door (already matched to one taken from her hair yesterday when she'd arrived at the prison); photographs the KGB had taken from Gazenko's desk drawer at the Institute — so wonderful that Galina had written "For Oleg" and then her name on the back of one! And finally, the two napkins with names and places penciled on them; the baker had provided this information willingly, and now these notes in his own handwriting made him the prosecution's primary witness.

Only one more task needed to be done: the baker must to be informed he would be required to testify against his wife and sister-in-law during their trial. Boris Petrov put on his overcoat and *ushanka*, preparing to leave his office. He'd promised the baker news by the end of the day. Now he was ready to deliver news, but of course it would not be what the baker was expecting. They had offered to send officers along with Boris, in case the baker offered resistance, but he'd declined the offer.

"We're neighbors," he'd assured them. "There will be no problem. I can do this alone."

The bakery was still closed and the handwritten sign was still stuck to the front door, but as he approached in the twilight hours, the barrister saw the baker sitting forlornly inside, an open bottle of vodka in one hand, staring out through the glass door panel. When he saw the barrister approaching, Victor jumped up and eagerly unlocked the door; the bells above it jingled merrily as he opened it wide.

"Please come in," he offered. "I've been waiting for you."

"Of course," Boris smiled. "I'm sorry I could not get here any sooner."

There has been a mistake made, the barrister proceeded to explain, once seated comfortably. They were not supposed to take the wife, only the sister, but once an arrest is made, it cannot be easily undone. He pulled an envelope from inside his coat, opened it and handed a single piece of paper to Victor. This is the quickest way to resolve the matter, the barrister continued. If you will sign this witness document, the trial can be scheduled immediately. I have been assured that the trial will be swift and the sentence light. Your wife will most likely be released into your custody and will serve any sentence under house arrest, rather than in prison. Because the charges against your sister-in-law are more serious, she will most likely be exiled, but not incarcerated. Both these women are very lucky that times have changed; there is no torture under Khrushchev. Prison is a much better place than it used to be.

The tired, befuddled and fully inebriated Victor thought he'd just heard the best news possible: his wife would be coming home and put under his supervision, and his sister-in-law would be sent to live far, far away. He only had one question.

"When will I see my Lilia again?"

"The sooner I can return this paperwork to the authorities, the sooner this will all happen."

Victor signed the paper and handed it back to the barrister.

"If you like, I could offer you a drink for all your help."

The barrister accepted the small glass of vodka Victor poured, downed it quickly and then left. Victor locked the bakery door, turned out the lights and sat back in his chair with the bottle of vodka, which he nursed the remainder of the night. When the morning light first appeared through the glass door of the bakery, he rose and rinsed his face with cold water, then decided it was time to bake again.

This is what I do, he thought to himself. I should maintain my routines, keep personal matters to myself, and present a good face to the public. Soon the sumptuous smells flowed throughout his shop and into the street. He took the "Sorry, We are Closed" sign down, smoothed his apron (since Lilia was not there to iron it for him) and set out the muffins and tarts for his customers.

"How is your family?" his customers would ask as they purchased morning treats from him.

"Doing very well, thank you," would be his truthful reply. The barrister had said so, and soon his Lilia would come home to him.

7.
Baikonur Cosmodrome

Activities in the control room were in full swing. Now that the R-7 and its precious payload stood vertically on the launch platform, surrounded by tall service towers, another full round of testing had to be completed before fueling and take-off. Most control room personnel were stationed at the banks of instrument panels, making notes of read-outs as they were received from the rocket and payload compartment. There was only one actual view of the launch area from this concrete bunker, built underground, 100 meters away, for protection during launch, and that was through a hand-cranked periscope mounted at the front of the room. Several men, including Number 20, took their turns looking into this instrument. The view, though limited, always increased one's excitement level: the missile in place meant that launch time was nearing, the spectacular event was eminent.

One area of the control room had been assigned to the biospace unit, and here Number 72 sat, as he had been sitting all through the night, leaning in close to the instrument panel, checking and re-checking every signal received from the dog in her cabin. The outdoor temperature had fallen dangerously low overnight, and, at his insistence, warm air had been pumped into the dog's cabin to keep her comfortable. Oxygen was entering the cabin as needed, and the carbon dioxide was being carried away. Her vital signs were excellent, as always. When she'd slept during the night, he'd been able to follow the data signaling her eye movements and tried to imagine the dreams she might be having. Briefly he wondered whether he'd appeared in her dreams.

Of course he'd understood everything she'd told him yesterday. More than anyone, this was a man finely tuned to understand the nuances of canine language: a series of gutteral pleas, small sighs, the occasional bark for punctuation, and all the accompanying body language. Plus, with Laika, those expressive eyes that dove directly into his soul whenever she made eye contact. Yesterday, she'd watched him intensely as she was carried away, and he'd stopped breathing until he reminded himself that he must start again.

Now he kept vigil over her remotely, on the tiny black-and-white television screen mounted right in front of him, oddly sliced into a series of slightly blurred, horizontal lines that refreshed themselves slowly to reveal slight movement: she folded her paws and rested her head on them; her delightful ears positioned themselves half up and half down as she strained to identify the noises around her. She seemed comfortable enough and had not yet complained or misbehaved. In fact, she was the perfect passenger so far, eating, sleeping, breathing normally and using the waste bag. Even the ever-vigilant Yazdovskiy, Number 58, had finally breathed a sigh of relief.

Number 20 had stopped by earlier to tell Number 72 that they would be testing the timer for the new Tral-D telemetry system today, to make sure it could be activated for fifteen minutes automatically during each hour and a half orbit around the Earth. Once in orbit, Laika's signals would be gathered and recorded constantly inside the spacecraft, but transmitted to Earth only during the fifteen-minute activation window. After the launch, Number 72 would have to adjust to not knowing how Laika was faring, except during these brief intervals.

This afternoon's test would darken his television screen, taking her away from him for more than an hour before returning her for a mere 15 minutes; he knew he'd soon have to get used to this cruelly intermittent schedule. As much as he'd come to adore the dog, as much as he needed time to anticipate and prepare for the pain he'd feel from her loss, and as much as he dreaded being out of touch with her for any time at all, Number 72 understood this was what the mission demanded. He knew he must do the job he'd been trained for, and he must keep the same promise she'd made to him. If she could be strong and sure, then he must rise to her performance level. He could not let her down; he must be the perfect partner for this adventure.

She was awake now, straining in her harness to take in everything around her, her movements stuttery, like a movie running at the wrong speed, but that was a factor of the television camera, not of its subject. Finally she looked up, directly into the television camera and cocked her head, staring inquisitively and then barking twice. She would not look away; eventually Number 72 had to turn himself away from her curiously determined gaze.

8.
Lubyanka Prison, Moscow

"Confess your crimes!"

Lilia sat cold and trembling in her thin prison gown, facing her first interrogator. She'd finally been taken out of her tiny box this morning, given a cold shower and the lightweight prison garb, water and a slice of bread to eat, and her number: 55905. She was so weak and fatigued that she did not think she could utter a sound in response. She could barely sit upright. This loud, uniformed man terrified her even more than Victor; she stared at him mutely, hoping to wrap herself in a silence that would somehow protect her, but she soon understood that silence would not be allowed.

"Confess your crimes, now!" he ordered her again, his voice increasing in volume and in urgency. She could not bear to watch his anger erupt. She must come up with an answer.

"The only thing I can think of," she began quietly, "is that I wanted a little dog of my own to keep me company."

"You wanted a dog?" The interrogator laughed harshly. "What kind of confession is this?"

"The dog I wanted," Lilia continued, "you see, her name is Kudryavka."

"So what?" The interrogator was impatient to get this worthless conversation over with.

"Don't you know who Kudryavka is?" She looked up at him in disbelief.

"Silence! I will ask the questions," he thundered. "Who is this Kudryavka?"

"She's the dog they've chosen to fly into space."

"Aha!" The interrogator sat up with renewed attention and began making copious notes. "So that's why you went to the Institute, to steal the government's property, yes?"

"They are planning to kill Kudryavka." Lilia listened to her own voice gaining confidence.

"You must answer my question!" he shouted, and her newfound courage evaporated.

"All I wanted to do was save her life." She began sobbing and would say no more.

The interrogator dismissed the weeping woman, whose uncontrolled emotion would now surely prevent her from saying anything more of value. He would take this time to discuss his findings with the prosecutor.

"We will talk again soon," he warned Lilia as she was led away from the interrogation room.

The hallways of the prison were narrow, with many turns. As the guards led Lilia back to her dreaded cell, she noticed them clicking their tongues as they approached every turn; she did not know this was their established signal to other guards that a prisoner was approaching. Great care was taken so that prisoners never saw one another; isolation was one of the tortures inflicted here (hunger, cold and the inability to sleep were among the others). The guards led her upstairs and back downstairs more than once, until she was hopelessly confused. She noticed that the stairwells all had suicide barriers made of heavy netting; no one would leap and die here, at least not by her own hand.

Then a surprise: Lilia was put in a new cell. This one was larger and had a low stool for sitting; one bare light bulb blazed high overhead, and in one corner rested a *parasha*, a welcome slop bucket which Lilia had to use right away. How strange that this horrible room could feel pleasant, she thought, gratefully sitting down and leaning against one wall, dropping almost immediately into a much-needed sleep.

9.
November 2
Baikonur Cosmodrome

Something was horribly wrong. I'd been locked inside this box long enough to eat and poop more than once, but no one had come around to praise me for it, nor to unlock the door and let me out. There had been no treats.

An occasional human (Number 11 or someone like him) had stopped by, but only to gawk. Upon arrival, the visitor would look at me through the round glass window, sometimes smiling, sometimes not, always making notes on a clipboard. *I'm fine,* I'd say to him, *but I'm ready to get out now, and have my treat.* But none of these humans understood a thing I said. Instead each one disappeared as suddenly as he'd shown up. All I could smell now was the air itself; all other odors of humans and their machines had been removed from my box. Sometimes the air felt warm; other times cool. Someone nearby must be adjusting the temperature, I decided, and I barked to get his attention, but he would not show himself.

Even though I was alone in this box, there were hints of myriad activities all around me: the sounds of pumps and fans moving the air about, gears turning and senseless signals beeping, a host of precision adjustments made by invisible hands to instruments hidden above my head. I'd become a part of the larger object I was attached to with wires and bags and sensors. Gradually I'd realized that the larger thing encompassing me was not just this box, but everything beyond it: the energy pulsing all around me, the activity I could hear going up and down whatever tower I sat atop, the voices of the men who worked here who would not open the door and let me out.

The next time I looked up, I noticed a tiny red light glowing just above my ears and became mesmerized by it. While the other sights and sounds in this place were transitory and without meaning to me, this little red light, I came to believe, was trying to tell me something. I just couldn't figure out what. I watched it constantly, until my neck became stiff from too much looking up. I whined and barked at it, hoping to generate some response, but there was nothing except its steady glow. I knew that it took humans to make lights shine, the way Poodle Girl or Gazenko used to shine lights into my mouth and ears. So, I reasoned, there must be someone behind the red light who'd eventually notice me and get me out of here. I must make myself be patient and of course I must continue to behave myself. I must also be vigilant; whenever I'd doze off, I'd soon wake myself up, just to check on the red light overhead, and there it was, the only sure thing, the only thing that had not abandoned me in this place.

Enough time had passed for the sky outside, which I could see through my little round porthole, to get dark and then light again, maybe more than once. I had to admit I was losing all track of time.

Eventually I'd come to believe this present moment would continue forever, and had relaxed into it; I'd even slept and dreamed once or twice — about Gazenko on the other end of the red light, trying to see inside my mouth, my ears, my soul.

Then suddenly the red light, the one that had glowed above my head with such consistency, went out. I sat there whining its loss until it came back on, but soon it went out again, and this time, no amount of whining would bring it back. I was beside myself with restless uncertainty. Even the red light could not be trusted. Things were changing; time had become operational once more, and this was not necessarily a good thing.

10.
November 3
Baikonur Cosmodrome

Number 20's relentless to-do list had dwindled to the last few items. Yesterday's glitch in the Tral-D system had been quickly repaired. He'd decided at the last minute to test one process that probably did not need to be tested, the telemetry timing unit, as it depended on the reliable, mechanical action of an old-fashioned alarm clock. But this was his mindset; unless it was tested, he could not be sure it would perform correctly.

First the Tral-D, which had been running continuously, had been turned off, then the timer turned on. In the control room, they'd waited for the timer to turn the telemetry back on, and it had, transmitting all the information that had been recorded while the Tral-D was off. After 15 minutes of operation, the timer had turned the telemetry off again, just as they'd anticipated. Before Number 20 would allow anyone to note this success, however, he'd instructed the workers that they must wait again now, for over an hour, to see if the timer would come on properly a second time. It was the 90-minute cycle that must be tested, not just the 15-minute timer, he'd explained. He could tell that some of the workers had little patience for such obsessiveness on his part, when there were so many other tests they must complete before the precious "launch" key could be inserted and turned. Restlessly they'd all waited, watching the control room's big clock on the front wall creep forward until it was time for the telemetry to be turned back on. But nothing had happened.

Rather than take advantage of what was clearly an "I-told-you-so" moment, Number 20 instead had called the man over who'd customized the alarm clock timer. He'd waved away this man's profuse apologies and told him to get out there and fix it; the man did, by climbing all the way up the scaffolding to the top of the rocket, opening the round silver orb where the timer had been installed, pulling it out and adjusting it right there up in the air. Then he'd re-installed it and in his hurried excitement to get word back to Number 20 that it should function properly now, he'd decided, foolishly, to leap to the ground rather than take the stairs or the elevator. He'd twisted his ankle seriously, but now the excruciating wait was worthwhile; the timer had worked, through three grueling cycles, and Number 20 seemed satisfied at last.

Early this morning, Number 20 had approved the start of the fueling process, the automatic pumping of 253 metric tons of liquid oxygen and kerosene into the core rocket and into the four boosters surrounding it, from nearby railroad cars that had been carefully moved into place overnight. This was the most critical operation leading up to launch, as the fuel was extremely combustible, and great care, and time, had to be taken. Two hours were required to fully load the R-7 with liquid propellant.

Once the fueling was underway, Number 20 made his usual rounds in the control room, visiting each work area and conferring with the men at each station; he'd hand-picked all control room workers and would allow no substitutes, even if one came down with a bad cold or woke up with a fever. His usual manner with the workers was formal and controlled, but today he'd relaxed slightly into someone friendlier. He knew what his workers needed most right now was confidence in all they'd learned and done up to this point; he hoped his own demeanor toward them would create the right atmosphere throughout the control room.

He stopped by the biospace work area and took a seat next to Number 72, who was staring at the darkened television screen; the Tral-D was in its off-cycle now. Both men were silent for a short time; then Number 20 spoke.

"There is one thing you still must do."

Number 72 was surprised; he'd been thorough and methodical while going through his final checklist, and every step had been successfully completed. He looked at Number 20 and waited.

"You should go now," Number 20 told him quietly, "and say good-bye."

Without waiting for an answer, Number 20 got up slowly and moved to the next work area, while Number 72 did as he'd been instructed — what the mission demanded. He left the underground control room and climbed the metal stairs leading to ground level, where he was met by one of the launch pad workers, who escorted him to the base of the massive R-7 missile. There he was put inside a tiny elevator that would carry him to the top of the missile, where Laika would be waiting. On the way up, he tried desperately to compose a properly inspiring speech of his own, the final words he'd deliver to his little Laika, but no fresh thoughts would enter his mind.

11.

Suddenly he appeared, just outside, peering in through the round window of my box. I jumped up, barked and wagged my tail in joy to greet him. He'd come to rescue me; I'd passed the test and now would be let out of this cramped little container! I could stretch my legs out in all directions, scratch the tortuous itch under my chin with my back paw, roll over and use the floor as a backscratcher, turn around and around chasing my own tail. They'd take these silly clothes off me, I'd be fed decent food, and I'd be able to poop wherever I pleased. Soon I'd see Albina again; I'd apologize and we'd kiss and make up. And from now on, I'd be a better dog: gentler, kinder, unselfish, less critical, and pleasant beyond belief. Honestly, I would. Just open the door.

But the door did not open. We looked at each other through the round window for a long time; then he placed one hand on its surface before turning away. I stretched my nose close toward the window, trying to smell what his hand was telling me, but the thick glass allowed nothing to pass through. It was as if he'd had one last notable thought, one more critical piece of advice to offer, and had come here only to find no way to transmit this information. He disappeared as suddenly as he'd appeared.

I heard a fresh bustle of human and mechanical activity outside, and sudden darkness descended all around me. I think I barked once, twice, then stopped trying because I knew no one was paying attention. A soft whir and pieces of the walls and floor rose toward me, stopping when they touched my ears and chin; I realized I could no longer move my head in any direction. I was trapped in one position, and could only look ahead into complete darkness as the thunderous, ear-splitting roar and horrendous shaking began.

12.

The R-7 looks like a big woman, someone on the launch crew (well outside hearing range of the boss) had remarked once the flaring boosters had been attached to the missile's central core and the whole contraption had been raised to a standing position. The boosters, near the bottom, are her full skirts, just touching the ground, and they'd set a fancy, pointed hat, the satellite's silver shroud, on top of her head. This afternoon, after standing there in her stiffly dignified pose for the past few days while they'd run their hands all over her, the tall lady in thick skirts suddenly catches on fire in all the right places.

For the second time ever, and in just under a month from the first time, Number 20 stationed himself at the periscope inside the blockhouse to watch a near-perfect launch. As with the last such event, the launch seemed barely to succeed at first, the entire missile and its support structures enveloped in the brilliant flames and thick exhaust bursting from underneath, as if they would all be consumed and incinerated. Then the ponderous missile, its boosters and the all-important payload crept upward slightly, struggling to escape the billowing smoke and the unrelenting gravity of Earth; whether or not there would be enough thrust to accomplish this feat would be known for sure within seconds.

The entire building trembled; a low-frequency roar pierced the thick concrete walls reinforced with iron, permeating the control room. Though there were no windows, there was the distinct sensation of a brilliant light flashing. No one spoke. No one seemed to be breathing. Time was nearly at a standstill.

Outside, the slow motion rising continued; now the shiny, pointed nose cone could be seen outdistancing the thick smoke, also rising, but spreading out on all sides as well, and throughout the fire pit underneath.

The tempo increased as the sluggish missile cleared the launch platform, and as it did so, the elegant support towers separated exactly as they were supposed to, lowering themselves to the ground on all sides.

"The flower has opened," someone in the control room called out. Sputnik 2 had begun its historic journey. With every moment passing, with each small increase in altitude, the hope growing among those monitoring the progress would not yet let itself be voiced.

Least of all would Number 20 allow himself to feel the relief or the joy of a successful launch; his nerves were drawn taunt, his mood clearly visible in the straight, thin set of his lips, the fierce drive in his dark eyes straining to envision the missile behaving perfectly all the way from the launch pad to its maneuver into orbit around the Earth.

If anyone had asked him about the space dog at this point, Number 20 might have returned a blank gaze. What dog? What I have been watching is a finely tuned system, a complex and monstrously sized machine, taking the next gigantic forward step toward the stars. The world's first space dog had become subsumed within the greater Soviet space effort, but what a spectacle it was, roaring and blazing its way into the bright blue sky. It would be in retrospect that the world would realize the importance of the small warm-blooded creature riding inside, testing the unknown for humans who would soon follow.

Only one person was watching the dog, and only the dog, during the thunderous ascent, his face so close to the television screen that his uneven breath condensed on its glassy surface. He scanned the uneven black-and-white images as they shook relentlessly and flashed off and then back on repeatedly. His throat was closed, his mind was blank and his body was tense all over, tuned to catch any clue provided about the canine passenger's status as the R-7 carried her away from him at 7.7 kilometers per second.

"Goodbye, Laika," Number 72 was finally able to say.

13.

You cannot imagine what these few minutes were like; no one could imagine it, because no one had experienced any of this before, although I suppose Albina had come close. She'd been right, of course, but she'd also been so, so wrong. I went up, straight up, and the more I went up, the more my body begged to stay on the ground. I was pushed so far down into my seat, I was sure I'd never be able to sit up again. I could not move any part of myself; I could not open one eye. Even my insides felt leaden.

At the same time I was shaken from side to side in the most intense vibration I'd ever experienced. My head was throbbing from the motion, and if it hadn't been held in place by whatever restraints they'd added at the last minute, I think it would have been wrenched completely off my neck.

There was still nothing but darkness to see, but the sounds I heard were amazing — whines, roars, quivers, and long resounding rumbles that got so loud I thought my sensitive doggie ears were going to burst. But I could also hear music in these sounds, and I wanted badly to add my two cents. I tried to bark, to whine or to howl, to participate in some way, but even a tiny whimper was not possible.

Just as in the torture room back at the kennel, but more so, I knew I'd have to give in eventually to the incredible heaviness, my feet like rocks that would not move, my stomach reeling from the relentless undertow. Even breathing was becoming nearly impossible. My brain was equally sluggish; I could not think a single coherent thought.

Just as I was about to pass mercifully into unconsciousness, the noise and shaking abruptly stopped, and the leaden weight inside me dissipated. Just as suddenly, I found I could once again bark, so I did, not just once, but over and over. I used all the barks in my vocabulary. *I am here*, I kept saying, *I am alive, and I have passed the next test. I deserve big treats for this, do I not?*

Soon I heard soft whirring on both sides of my head, and the devices that had held my head and neck in place departed. Now I found I could shake my head back and forth, and so I did, with enthusiasm. My head felt light as a wind-blown snowflake as it bobbled about, but that was only the beginning. I watched in amazement as my entire body rose until I was no longer touching my seat. I was floating! Only the chains they'd attached to my vest kept me from flying off in all directions. My paws hovered in front of my face; even when I tried, I could not convince them to touch the seat below me. I gulped in mouthfuls of air, pleased to be breathing normally again.

Hadn't Albina predicted this part, too? I strained to remember what she'd said would happen next. Oh yes, I'd be jumping out of the box and floating back down to Earth soon, where someone would be waiting to catch me. This was almost over. I'd be back home soon.

I relaxed at last; I must have floated off to sleep then, invisibly cushioned all around by nothing more than the air itself.

14.

Later that day, the thrilling news came over Radio Moscow.

"The Soviet Union has launched the first living creature into the cosmos.

"A dog, described as a female mixed breed, was projected into space this morning aboard the artificial space satellite Sputnik 2. Sputnik 1, launched on October 4th, is still circling the globe.

"The dog, hermetically sealed in a container equipped with an air-conditioning system and fitted with monitors to check heartbeat and other vital signs, was reported to be calm during the first hours of the historic flight.

"Sputnik 2, launched to commemorate the 40th anniversary of the October Revolution, weighs 508 kilograms and carries instruments for studying solar and cosmic rays, temperature and pressure, two radio transmitters and oxygen and food supplies for the historic first space passenger. The satellite is traveling nearly 1,500 kilometers above the Earth — higher than Sputnik 1 — and is orbiting at a speed of about 8 kilometers a second. It will take one hour and 42 minutes to circle the Earth. The satellite is transmitting telegraphic signals that are being picked up by receiving stations around the globe."

"Truly amazing." Victor shook his head as he listened to the radio in his bakery while boxing up today's left-over baked goods.

"She's in outer space now," the priest said, equally in awe, looking upward as he nibbled a complimentary after-hours fruit tart and offered a silent prayer for the dog's safe travel and return to Earth.

"You speak as if you know this space dog, Father," Victor joked with his visitor.

"As do you — of course you remember the little dog Kudryavka?"

Victor laughed out loud. "And where would I have met this...Kudryavka?"

Dumbfounded by Victor's professed ignorance, the priest stopped chewing; several crumbs fell from his lips to the bakery counter.

"You truly do not know?"

"Know what?" Victor's laughter evaporated.

The priest pointed heavenward. "That this is the same little dog your wife worried so much about, the little stray that used to live in this neighborhood?"

Victor was incredulous. "The bitch my wife wanted to adopt — that's the space dog?"

The priest nodded. Victor stared into the shadows gathering in the street outside his shop, growing uncharacteristically quiet and contemplative. The priest thought it best to leave the baker with his thoughts, whatever they were, so he pocketed his half-eaten tart, picked up the two boxes Victor had prepared, said a soft goodbye and hurried away.

"Goodbye, Father," Victor had mumbled automatically as the priest departed. "Thank you for coming and please come again."

The priest had begun these evening visits after Lilia and her sister had been arrested. As much as he deplored the baker and the way his politics and ineptitude had caused two innocent women to be incarcerated, he hoped he might offer comfort and possibly some wise counsel to Victor that might eventually help free the sisters.

It had been his idea, for instance, to take end-of-the-day baked goods to the prison; he knew prisoners there were rarely provided sufficient meals, usually only watery soup and a thin slice of bread each day; only those lucky enough to get boxes from the outside to augment this meager diet did not go hungry. Victor had resisted, however, remembering the barrister's threat; he feared being arrested himself if he showed his face at Lubyanka.

"You package them in two small boxes and write the names on them," the priest suggested, "and I will take them to Lubyanka. If they haven't arrested me by now," he reasoned out loud, "I'm most likely safe."

In truth, the priest, like Victor, was terrified of going anywhere near the prison. He still had nightmares about the men who'd terrorized him, wrecked his home and frightened his parishoners, but he prayed for courage to do the right thing for the two women, who'd done nothing wrong. He decided to remove his cleric's collar for the trip downtown, dressing instead in a woolen shirt and pants, his winter overcoat, and wearing his big black cowboy hat low above his face to further protect and disguise him. He was immediately pleased that nobody on the Metro called him "Father" or offered him a seat out of deference to his religious rank. It was a joyous masquerade; he felt like another man altogether: a Hollywood cowboy rushing toward certain heroism and a carefully-scripted happy ending.

While on the train, thinking over the incredible news he'd heard today, he got the idea of hiding messages inside the treats. He must send both Lilia and her sister news of the dog now in space; prisoners were not usually provided up-to-date information about events in the world outside. He dug into his pocket for the note paper and pencil he always carried; his memory sometimes failed him, so he'd gotten in the habit years ago of writing down the specific names and prayer requests of his parishioners. Once he reached his destination, he sat on a bench near the Lubyanka station, thoughtfully composing his tiny notes.

He'd opened each box carefully. There were five treats inside Lilia's box, and four in her sister's. Shouldn't he hide messages inside each treat? What else could he say? These little compositions were like miniature sermons, he decided; everything must be said in the fewest words possible, but the recipients of his words should be comforted in their current situation, and they must also have renewed faith in the future. He did not know Lilia very well at all, and had never met the sister, whose name he now knew to be Galina; Victor had printed it on the outside of her box. He decided to send Victor's wife a note that might provide her with much needed hope and comfort, and the same for Galina, except her note must also create renewed determination. She was the more secular of the sisters, he knew, but because she was more world-wise, she might be able to come up with some plan for their defense.

When all was said and done, he'd created a series of messages, inserting one in each treat. He was proud of his work, especially the extra one he'd composed for Lilia, the one he considered to be his first love letter. No matter that she would think it was from Victor; this very special note would warm her all the same, and that was the goal, was it not?

The priest stood tall and proud, adjusted the angle of his cowboy hat and strode boldly and purposefully with his boxes toward the front door of the big yellow prison.

15.
Lubyanka Prison, Moscow

By now, each sister had been separately interrogated several more times. Each time, a written confession was read out loud and the sister was asked to sign it. Galina's "confession" was her acknowledgement of engaging in subversive activity designed to undermine the Soviet space program, stealing official government documents (the TASS photographs found in the apartment, matching the ones found at the Institute), and using the stolen articles to incite her sister to join in the subversive activity.

"These are serious charges you face," the interrogator told her. "You could be put to death for doing any one of these things."

He paused to let his words make an impression on her before continuing. "But if you sign this confession, you may very well be able to save your own life."

Try as he might, the interrogator could not persuade Galina to sign any document presented to her, and each time would have to send her back to her cell without a confession. At the end of each interrogation, she'd demand information about her sister, shouting as she was being led from the interrogation room. Her demands were ignored.

She'd also asked for paper and pencil each time, and had written a series of letters, addressed to Dr. Oleg Gazenko at the Institute of Aviation and Space Medicine, begging him to intercede for her and her sister; she suspected these letters never left Lubyanka Prison.

Lilia's confession was more complex; the quieter sister, she'd admitted to very little so far, yet the interrogator had high hopes for this session, as she was led in and seated before him.

"I have something here I'd like for you to read," he said, passing a document to her. "You will see that your husband has denounced you, has validated the criminal charges against you, and has agreed to testify against you at your trial."

Lilia took time to read the brief statement and then to examine the signature beneath it; this was her husband's handwriting, she was sure. She looked up in disbelief as the interrogator handed her a second document.

"Now will you sign your confession?"

Later, back in her cell, Lilia wished she'd had more time to think things over before signing anything. She could not believe Victor would betray her this way; true, he was sometimes angry with her, but always he apologized and told her he loved her afterwards. He would not have agreed with the paper he'd signed unless someone had forced him to do this, or had told him lies and made him believe them. She doubted whether there was any way to rescind her confession, however. Now she'd have to wait, wait, wait, to find out what would happen next.

Suddenly there was activity outside her cell; the small peephole slid open.

"Step away from the door now," someone ordered her.

Lilia stepped backwards as far as she could go. The door to her cell opened a crack, just wide enough to slide a small brown paper package inside.

"From the outside," was the only explanation; she took the package and the door slammed shut again.

She ripped the string from a shoebox that looked familiar, and opened the box to find a lovely collection of her husband's baked goods inside! Having had no food since the slice of bread early this morning, she grabbed a lemon muffin, her favorite, took a huge bite, then spit it back out. She'd bitten into a piece of folded paper inside the muffin; she unfolded the paper and held it directly under the light bulb over her head to read "You are beloved" carefully printed in tiny block letters, as if someone were trying to disguise his handwriting.

Thoughtfully, she refolded the paper and hid it in her shoe, then finished the muffin, wondering whether the other sweets contained similar notes. Wisely, she decided she must ration herself; tomorrow morning she'd allow herself another treat, and perhaps be surprised by another message. Someone must have tricked Victor into signing the paper they showed me, she reasoned, just as they have tricked me. Such comfort and renewed hope allowed her to sleep through the night.

In her cell, Galina was handed a similar package "from outside," without further information. Inside the blueberry muffin she chose to eat first was a folded note. She opened it to read: "Your sister is nearby." Then she quickly tore into the remaining treats, where she found additional messages: "Dog alive in space." "There is a way out." "The answer will come to you."

Unlike her sister, Galina stayed awake all night long, her hope renewed, but also her determination. She sat thoughtfully on her stool under the harsh white light bulb, trying to imagine the series of chess moves she must successfully make to save her sister and herself.

16.
Earth Orbit

My freedom — and my enlightenment — arrived in several distinct phases. First the blessed silence; then no more being shaken all over, and my release from the restraints that had locked my head in one place; now I could look up, down and all around, but still there was nothing except darkness to see. Soon, however, I heard a gentle mechanical sound just outside my box. A sudden jolt, a sense of being pushed backward, a loud click and then a quiet release. Suddenly I could see out my porthole, the most amazing sights filling my unbelieving eyes!

It was nighttime and there were stars everywhere, big, crisp, shiny stars, like the grand show in the sky the night Gazenko had taken me for a drive, only closer and brighter now, shining so clearly and so insistently, I think I could have grabbed one if the door had opened.

How could Albina have not mentioned these exquisite stars, I wondered, but then perhaps she'd traveled during the daytime. I could hardly wait now to see her again, so I could tell her everything that had happened. She should be here herself; we were supposed to travel together, but maybe, I mused, she'd taken a different flight. I searched the night sky outside my porthole, hoping to see another box floating nearby, dear Albina looking out her own porthole, suddenly seeing me and yelping in delight, but as far as I could see in any direction, there were stars and more stars, but no more boxes.

Looking at so many stars was making me dizzy, so I closed my eyes and tried to make sense of what I'd seen. I was not looking up at stars overhead as I'd done on Earth, but moving among them. There were stars above and below me, and on all sides surrounding me in my box. If I was traveling among the stars which used to hang over my head, that must mean I was no longer on the ground. Not only was I floating; so was the box I was riding in, along with the stars I saw outside. I let the wonder wash over me, trying hard to understand, until practical matters intervened. A pellet of food appeared, then began mysteriously to float away from me; quickly I grabbed it in my mouth and gulped it down, used the poop bag, then fell asleep.

17.

Predictably, news about the launch of Sputnik 2 took the world by storm, and Galina's former colleagues at the news bureau soon were pressed for details. Most questions were not about the scientific instruments aboard, nor the research they might conduct in space, but about the canine passenger now flying high above the Earth. Suddenly the space race had a heartbeat, and the soft thump, thump, thump — as well as the mechanical beep, beep, beep that had first been associated with Sputnik 1 — could be picked up by tracking stations around the world. Soon the world — especially the international news outlets — clamored for more information.

What kind of dog? How big? How old? What breed? What is the dog's name? How would the dog eat in space, or breathe? How long would the dog remain in orbit above the Earth? How would they get the dog safely back to Earth?

An exuberant Khrushchev had learned his lessons well from the first Sputnik, and now wasted no time in harnessing the Soviet propaganda machine to propel the newest Soviet space success into glorious news stories lauding the superiority of the Soviet Union. Give them plenty of what they want, he ordered the TASS director.

Answer their questions. Send them excellent news about the space dog.

The immediate problem was that no one at TASS had answers to the questions being asked, so the news bureau director put a long distance telephone call through to the Baikonur Cosmodrome. Once he'd made it clear that he'd been instructed by Khrushchev himself to make these inquiries, he was eventually handed over to a nameless doctor (his identification was not permitted, either by name or number, in this top-secret situation) who, he was assured, had been involved in launching the space dog.

The doctor who eventually picked up the telephone, Number 72, was in no mood to talk to the press. When the call had come, he'd had his hands full in the control room. The spacecraft had found its way into an elliptical orbit around the Earth, and just minutes ago, the protective shroud had been successfully jettisoned. Whatever else was happening to Laika, he thought, at least now she'd have a grand view. He could not monitor her current condition; the first transmission was over and the next one not scheduled for at least half an hour. Her vital signs as transmitted during the launch itself showed that her heartbeat had increased dramatically, but under those circumstances, whose heartbeat wouldn't? He'd predicted that once she became weightless, her heartbeat would return again to a normal rate. He assured a worried Number 58 that she'd calm down quickly once the noise and shaking had stopped, just as she always had during tests at the kennel. But until he knew this absolutely, he could not relax.

That's when Number 20 had come over, insisting that 72 take a few minutes to answer some questions from the news bureau; this was what the mission demanded, 72 was reminded. Number 20 was well aware of the space dog's vital signs as transmitted during the first orbit, and he recognized Number 72's understandable distress about them.

"Besides," Number 20 added, "a walk in the fresh air will do you good."

"Yes, what can I do for you?" Number 72 said, somewhat irritably, into the special telephone he'd walked to another building to answer, the only long-distance connection at the Cosmodrome, and not a very good one at that. He listened carefully to each question asked and tried to provide an answer, but with such a bad connection, he could not be sure the man on the other end of the telephone was getting the information accurately.

"Her name is Kudryavka," he spoke in a loud, slow voice.

"Please, could you repeat that?"

Even after spelling it twice, the man from the news bureau had not understood.

"I'm sorry," he apologized, "but we need the name of the dog."

Number 72 was out of patience. If they wanted a name, he'd give them one they could at least spell.

"It's Laika," he shouted into the telephone receiver. "L-A-I-K-A."

"Got it," the reporter acknowledged. "Laika it is. That is her breed?"

"That is her name!"

Then he saw someone signaling him from the door-way.

"I'm sorry, but I have to go now." He hung up the receiver and hurried toward the blockhouse, pleased to have an excuse, any excuse, to get back to work.

"Please check these temperature readings," Number 58 handed him several sheets of paper as soon as Number 72 returned to the biospace work area.

"Too high." Number 72 recognized the problem im-mediately. "When's the next transmission?"

"Still twenty minutes away."

Number 72 turned the adjustment knobs on the tele-vision screen; stubbornly it remained dark. No data was coming in now, and the last set was nearly an hour old. Rising temperature in the dog's cabin could pose a seri-ous problem, but the cabin also had a cooling fan auto-matically set to kick on if the temperature increased too much. Damn this Tral-D, Number 72 cursed the telemetry system that stubbornly refused to let him check on Laika when she so obviously needed him. He'd have to wait for the fresh data, which would come to him according to the schedule. It was the only thing he could do.

18.

I'm back in my old neighborhood, watching the sunrise, pleased to have survived another impossibly cold night. No one is around to bother me, so I stretch myself out in a sunny spot on the sidewalk, but I've never known the sun to behave so strangely. A burst of blinding light rapidly envelops me, scorching my tender nose and the tips of my ears. It's time to move into the cool shadows, but I can't. I'm stuck to the sidewalk.

I was awake. The stars had vanished and daytime was pushing itself into every corner of my box. I blinked and barked, a little irritated at its insistence. Inside the box it was getting warm quickly, so I worked myself, by pulling with my teeth at my restraints, over to one side of the porthole as much as I could, hoping to escape the direct rays, but it was still hot. Fortunately the sun was on the move, quickly crossing the front of my box, then passing overhead. The morning ended quickly, giving way to an equally brief and intense afternoon. I could no longer see the sun, now behind me, but instead I saw something far more extraordinary: a soft blanket far below, decorated with dark irregular shapes, and scattered white wispy splotches and tentacles stretching in all directions. This blanket was curled into a rounded shape, as if covering a big ball that was moving, turning in place, it seemed, to provide a continually shifting pattern beneath me.

I was accustomed to having my feet below my body, planted securely on the ground (unless I'd rolled over, legs in the air, using the ground as a handy backscratcher), but here it was hard to figure out exactly what was up and what was down. I knew I'd traveled up into the sky; just how far up I was not sure. Logically, if the sun was above me, then what was down below should be solid, flat ground, the mostly gray place where I'd gone for a walk with Gazenko just before being locked away. But the sun was on the move and here was this strange curved blanket — could this be the place I'd come from? Of all the places I'd been in my short little life — my neighborhood, the kennel, the place Gazenko had driven me to, and the place I'd just been with Albina and Mushka — none of them looked like this.

I watched until lunch was served (or dinner — I had to admit I was a little confused about mealtimes by now); a soft whirring sound and a food lozenge showed up near my feet and rose slowly into the air; I was hungry, so I gobbled it up quickly before it floated away, wondering briefly why nothing stayed put anymore.

Then I thought about the other strange sensation I'd noticed, the one about time. Since I'd been put into this box, time itself had been behaving crazily, sometimes not advancing at all, and now, moving so quickly that I'd actually seen the sun hurrying across the sky. Time had slowed down and then sped up, but why?

As if to answer my question, the sky outside my box dipped into darkness and the big, bright stars jumped into my face again. I was so close to them that I must be far away from places I'd been before. My trip had taken me nearer to the stars, and here they looked different —

shiny, not twinkly — and enormous. So traveling a great distance made familiar things look odd and all out of proportion. The view from my window — not only the stars, but also the sun and the blanket — must be views from afar, brand new perspectives.

Then another mental leap and I grasped at the rest. If the sun and the shadows it cast had crept slowly before, but now moved much faster, then the way time passed must have changed for me, also. At first I'd been in this box for a long time, sitting still, and time seemed to sit still with me. Then we'd begun moving again, me in my box, faster and faster, and now time had sped up, also. Up here, time was not a constant thing you could use to plan your mealtimes and naptimes, but something that followed its own mysterious tempo, hurrying to arrange the sun, the stars and the blanket into surprising new views and sequences. Even as the blanket dimmed into darkness, sprinkled with a few stars of its own, I saw a brilliant light spreading over one edge of it. It was tomorrow already.

Instinctively I wondered whether it was time to sleep, to eat, or to poop. Then I realized it didn't matter; I was no longer bound by time, nor by any place I'd been before now. I was floating in my box, which was also floating; we were no longer attached to the ground underneath or to the time I'd spent there. I'd come unconnected from all I'd ever seen or done; I was sampling all times and all places simultaneously, on the grandest scale imaginable.

I wanted a name for this place I'd traveled to, how it behaved and what I was doing here, as if calling it by name would help me understand more. I remembered what Gazenko and Poodle Girl had called me back at the kennel, once I'd won the contest: "space dog." Now I knew what a space dog was, what a space dog did, and finally, what the contest had been about the whole time. This was space, the grand prize. I'd been awarded something that no one, not even Albina, herself a mere rocket dog, could have predicted: unrestricted, unbounded, unimaginable freedom.

But not, as it turns out, without a price.

19.

Victor was so distraught when he realized what all he'd caused that he sat upstairs, resting his arms on the kitchen table and weeping for half an hour.

Because he had not wanted the nuisance of a stray mutt hanging around, upsetting his customers, his Lilia was now in prison. Because he would not allow her to adopt the little stray when she'd asked, she'd let her sister talk her into some crazy scheme to get the dog anyway, and now both of them were accused of subversive activity against the government. Because he'd selfishly sold information about the dog to the government scientists, now here was a little dog that could have been Lilia's special pet zooming about in a Sputnik. Outer space was no place for a dog, he thought, and prison was no place for his dear wife.

The barrister had visited earlier today, to purchase two golden muffins, just as he used to do each morning, and to assure Victor once again that his wife and her sister were fine.

"They are kept warm and fed well," he'd said. "Lubyanka is not such a terrible place to be."

Victor no longer felt like pretending, but sensed he must proceed with great care and continued deference, at least until he got the information he so desperately needed.

"That's not what I've heard," he'd replied cautiously. "I've heard that the prisoners get very little food to eat, that they live in cramped cells with no heat or sunlight. They get showers once a week, in cold water only."

"You must not believe all that you hear," the barrister had said. "You must believe what I tell you, because I've been there and have seen it for myself."

But when pressed, the barrister could provide no further details on the condition of his wife and sister-in-law, nor could he say for sure when Lilia's trial would be scheduled, only that it would be soon.

"Will I be able to see her then?"

"Of course you can attend the trial," the barrister had promised. Victor wanted to know more; he'd invited the barrister to sit and visit for a while, but his guest got a sudden twitching in his arm and began toying nervously with his goatee.

"You must excuse me for running off," he'd told Victor, explaining that he must attend to an urgent task in his office next door. He'd just stopped by to let Victor know that things were proceeding efficiently, and that it would not be long until he'd see his wife again.

"At the trial, yes?"

"I can promise you, my friend," the barrister had smiled as he left the bakery, "that the trial will not start without you."

When he'd locked himself inside his old office next door, Boris Petrov worked quickly to gather whatever papers and files he'd need. He'd stuffed these materials into a worn leather briefcase and left the office, locking the door behind him. He would not be returning to this neighborhood. His work here was finished.

Outside, he'd hurried into a waiting sedan.

"What a fool that is next door," he'd remarked to the driver, just before closing the sedan door, forgetting for an unfortunate moment how quickly the buildings in this neighborhood had been built, with thin walls and no insulation.

Just inside the bakery door, Victor had watched and listened, his round face flushed and burning with shame.

"What a fool," he'd agreed.

Later that night, after weeping until he'd exhausted himself, unable to sleep, eat or think of anything beyond how foolish he'd been all along, and how gullible he'd been to believe the barrister's lies, he stuffed fresh underwear and an extra sweater into a duffle bag, left the apartment and headed to the Metro station to find whatever train would take him farthest away from his misery.

His "Sorry, We Are Closed" sign was once more posted on the bakery door and this time he would not remove it.

20.

When asked by the news bureau reporter about how long the dog would be in space and how she would return to Earth, Number 72 had noted that this information was classified for security reasons, and he could not divulge such facts. Number 20 had instructed him to say this.

"Tell them all is proceeding as planned," Number 20 had advised. "The dog is comfortable and is behaving normally, eating, barking, moving about."

Both 72 and 20 had noted the dog's condition during the most recent 15-minute transmission, which had just ended. The heat and humidity inside her cabin were higher still and she seemed agitated, straining at her restraints, barking repeatedly into the camera, but she was most definitely still alive. So far her weightlessness seemed to have caused no ill effects, and both her heartbeat and breathing were back within acceptable parameters.

"But we know she will die," Number 72 had replied angrily.

"How can we say for sure?" Number 20 had replied. "I should have died in the gulag, yet here I am. We do not know the end of the story. We can only report what we know. What we know now is that she is alive and well."

"This afternoon one Soviet scientist said that the animal's life was 'assured,'" *The New York Times* reported.

Pressured by his boss, Number 72 continued to provide information to the news bureau, and the news bureau continued to release updates on Sputnik 2 and its famous canine passenger to the rest of the world, not always with the greatest accuracy.

"Name of Satellite Dog Breeds Confusion Here," a British newspaper headline admitted. "Little is known about the dog except by those closely connected with the Soviet satellite project. Even its name and its sex have been kept secret.

"Laika, the name provided by TASS and the State Committee for Cultural Relations With Foreign Countries, is also the name of a breed of Soviet hunting dog, according to *The Great Soviet Encyclopedia*. Whether the dog Laika is actually a member of this breed is not known.

"The word 'laika' also means 'barker' in Russian."

The stray dog Kudryavka who'd barked into a microphone just a few days earlier on Radio Moscow had vanished from history; she'd been replaced by the heroic and high-flying Laika.

21.

When the red light blinked on again, I was ready and eager to explain all I'd seen and done, and all I'd thought of, as the world's first space dog. I described this place called space in great detail. I explained how the sun, stars and my home looked from space, and how oddly they behaved.

I'd figured out what the mission demanded of me: the red light was not (as I'd assumed earlier) trying to tell *me* something; I was supposed to tell *it* everything, information that may somehow be preserved and carried back to the time and place I'd come from. As with all lights, there had to be humans at the other end of this one, turning it on and off, just like the men who'd once visited my kennel, asking whether I'd say a little something for the radio audience.

"I believe she might," Gazenko had answered confidently, but I could smell his uncertainty; instinctively I knew this radio was a test we both must pass and I knew exactly how to do it.

I'd barked for them all. Gazenko's anxiety had changed to joy. Now I barked for them again, hoping Gazenko was with the men on the other end of the red light, and that he'd be as happy with me now as he'd been the day he first named me "Laika."

I knew my barks had a long way to travel and was not at all sure they would reach their destination. But I was certain Gazenko and I were still working together, and with great relief, I felt my own version of unrestrained joy leaking quietly into my butt bag.

I looked hard out my window at the blanket below, and could almost see him standing there now, on top of the tower where I'd last seen him, pulling his notepad from his pocket, waiting to catch my barks when they arrived.

22.

During the third orbit came the third transmission, with the dog's agitated performance. Watching the small television screen with all the brainpower he could muster, Number 72 strained to fill in blanks between the low-resolution images and slow transmission speed that provided disjointed slices of Laika's message from space, a series of barks, whines, whimpers, and dancing dark eyes insisting that he pay close attention. He was working feverishly to get it all, in canine; there was no time for human translation.

Suddenly the screen went dark, even though fifteen minutes had not passed.

"I need the picture!" Number 72 shouted frantically to everyone working in the control room. He had no idea who among them might be able to restore the television transmission, but someone must. This was too important to be missed. He stared at the blank screen, his anxiety increasing.

"Television signal's failed," someone shouted from across the room, jiggling buttons and turning knobs in vain.

Only Number 20 was not surprised to hear this news. As he'd anticipated, the loose connection on the camera had come completely apart, and no repair would be possible. He knew they would not see the space dog again. More importantly, the flight of the world's first space passenger would not end in tragedy — at least not the way they saw it.

23.

I'd done my job. I'd performed flawlessly, in fact, but I no longer expected treats for my services. There were no doggie treats in space, only the sun, the stars and the faraway blanket I could not touch or smell.

Neither was there going to be any homecoming for me. I would not be floating back down to the ground, and no one was waiting there to catch me. I'd traveled too far, too fast, and so much had changed that I knew no retracing of my route would be possible. If some human had shown up suddenly beside me, throwing the door open and saying, "You can go home now," I wouldn't have known where to start.

The red light, my only remaining connection to the place I'd come from, had disappeared again and this time did not return. No more looking or barking into it would be necessary, I thought, with some relief. I was tired, and longed for a good night's sleep — *my* idea of night, not the quick one passing by outside — but my box was so hot now, I could only float listlessly, hovering just above my seat, desperate for some relief. My brain felt sluggish; my tongue hung dry outside my mouth.

The sky outside went dark and then burst into light again. Eventually, as in the torture room back home, I knew I'd give in to what I could not control. I'd close my eyes, fall asleep, and would not wake up for a very long time.

Suddenly Albina appeared, wedged beside me in the impossibly small box and together we marveled over everything we'd seen and heard.

"I wasn't upset with you," she whispered. "I was worried about you. He's not to be trusted, you know."

I leaned closer to sniff; she was telling the truth.

"But you're crazy about him," I reminded her.

"No, just pretending." She offered a small sad smile. "I wanted out as much as you did. Actually I don't like him at all."

I was amazed by her unabashed confession. "You were just pretending?"

"Just like you," she leaned against my shoulder. "You *were* just pretending, weren't you?"

No, I wasn't. But never would I admit it, not even to my very best friend.

24.

The next time she was walked through the hallways of Lubyanka, clicking her tongue just to irritate the guards she was imitating, and into the interrogation room, Galina made a surprising request.

"I'm ready for my trial," she told the interrogator with a confident smile.

In the courtroom, facing the judge and that deceitful man who'd pretended to practice law in the office next door to the bakery, Galina laid out the facts she insisted would exonerate her.

The dog Kudryavka, the one she and her sister were accused of trying to steal from the government, did not exist. There was no dog with that name in the kennel, nor was this the dog that had been sent into space; the space dog's name was Laika, not Kudryavka. There were newspaper reports to verify this fact.

(She'd gotten tiny scraps of newspaper, hidden inside a strawberry tart, enough to allow her to plot her way out of this situation.)

"You might save yourselves some time and trouble by deciding my sister's fate now, in addition to mine," she'd advised them before continuing with her own defense. "After all, she and I are in this together."

As far as her sister was concerned, the citizen witness who'd signed the papers accusing her of similar crimes was not present to testify against her; he'd disappeared, and no one knew where he had gone.

But we must consider the hard evidence, Boris Petrov had countered. What about the hairpin found at the kennel? It's the same kind of hairpin we found in your sister's hair when she was arrested.

Go outside and pull a hairpin from any woman you find on the street, Galina replied. They're all the same. In the stores where we must shop, there is only one type of hairpin available for purchase. She was correct.

We have the photographs you signed and gave to Dr. Oleg Gazenko, stolen government property. Can you explain this?

Galina took a deep breath. This was the most serious charge she'd have to defend herself against. She hoped she'd have the courage to proceed with the story she'd prepared in repsonse to the question she'd known she'd be asked.

"Oleg Gazenko was my lover," Galina confessed in a quiet voice. "But of course we had to keep this fact secret. Not even my sister knows this. Not even the doctor's assistant knew. That's why she was so surprised to see me at the kennel that she called the police.

"He'd asked me to come there, of course, to say goodbye before he went away to launch the space dog," Galina continued. "We had to meet in secret, at odd times, and that night Korinna was not supposed to be on duty."

Galina offered the outrageous lie she'd just told with assuredness, betting on the fact that even if Gazenko were asked and even if he denied such an affair, this would only add credence to her claim that their liaison must be kept secret — and then at least Oleg would know what had happened to her.

Oleg Gazenko must be asked, of course. The judge paused the legal proceedings and placed a long distance telephone call to the Cosmodrome. Once more Number 72 was summoned from his duties to field another set of questions he did not want to answer.

"It is really not appropriate for you to be asking about my private life," he cautioned the judge, his raised voice crackling amid the long-distance static. When told about the charges facing Galina and her sister, he insisted that the women be released immediately.

"They have done nothing wrong," he admonished the judge. "The one named Galina was welcome to visit the kennel any time, on my authority. The fact that she brought her sister along is of no concern. Her sister is a simple housewife who loves dogs, that's all. Now please, are we finished now, because I really must get back to my work."

Only one more question, the judge persisted. "Is there a dog in the kennel named Kudryavka?"

"There is no dog anywhere with that name," Number 72 snapped back at his inquisitor.

The judge hung up the telephone, certain now, because of Gazenko's vehement denial, that the woman on trial must be the doctor's secret lover, the very doctor that had just sent a living creature into outer space, a dog named Laika, the very dog the whole world was now in love with. He did not think he could afford to interrupt the glory of the Soviet space program just to convict this — he had to admit — bold and beautiful woman calmly awaiting her fate in his courtroom.

Galina's best defense, the one she did not even know about, the one that ended up saving her and her sister, was her unabashed fearlessness, which so unnerved the authorities that they paused to consider her case more carefully than most. Given the current situation and the uneasy link between the sisters and the Soviet space program, the judge and his own legal counsel decided that a stiff sentence would not be appropriate. Galina and Lilia were each sentenced to five years only, to be served under house arrest. They were not to leave Moscow during this time, and they must report daily to an officer of the court. Boris Petrov, much to his chagrin, was appointed by the judge to oversee the sisters' house detention. His office was moved once again, from Lubyanka back to his old neighborhood, a more convenient place for him to carry out his new duties.

25.

On its third orbit around the Earth, Tral-D had sent increasingly garbled information during its 15-minute transmission. Since then, visual tracking of the satellite had confirmed that one section of the R-7 rocket, the long, skinny core, had not separated from the satellite as planned, perhaps causing problems in the spacecraft's temperature regulation system, which would affect not only the canine passenger, but possibly some of the delicate equipment on board as well. The television camera had stopped recording during the third orbit, and when the satellite passed overhead on its fourth orbit late that night, there was no Tral-D transmission at all.

Number 20 sighed deeply as he left the control room for the first time since the launch, to climb the stairs to the surface and to take a solitary walk underneath the stars. He was thinking already about how this mission would be interpreted in Soviet history: another grand success, no doubt, and one that would insure his continuing work on missile and satellite design and space exploration. The satellite had achieved Earth orbit and its passenger had survived, as far as they had been able to track her. Neither the extreme G-forces during launch nor the period of sustained weightlessness had caused any negative effects on the dog; all transmissions received indicated that she was behaving normally. She'd been the perfect choice: well trained, and once launched into space, she'd remembered all her training. Number 20 must remember to commend Number 72 on his superb work with the space dog, but not just now.

Number 72 sat forlornly by himself in the biospace work area. There was nothing more he could do, no more data to analyze, no pictures or sounds pulsing from afar, no more reports to compile, no connection with the spacecraft at all. Laika was truly on her own now. He refused to think of her death; with no hard evidence to prove she had perished, he stubbornly kept her alive in his thoughts, as it turned out, forever.

26.

That evening, Lilia was fetched from her cell at Lubyanka, given her own clothes to put on, then put in the back seat of a black sedan and driven home by a stone-faced man who would not answer any of her questions. Overjoyed but mystified, she stood in front of the bakery, which was closed, and looked up to see lights on in the upstairs apartment. Victor must be waiting there for her! She must look a mess, she realized suddenly, so she ran her hands through her hair and pinched both cheeks to make them red before going around back and climbing the stairs.

Galina was in the kitchen, stirring a pot on the stove. When she saw her sister, she dropped the spoon and ran to welcome Lilia home.

"I made soup," she announced, "but not very good soup, I'm afraid."

"No matter," Lilia replied, hugging her sister tightly, but then releasing her to walk about the apartment in search of someone else. "But where is Victor?"

"No one seems to know. He's disappeared."

"But he sent treats to me in prison," Lilia said. "With little messages inside."

"Your good Communist husband sent me treats as well," Galina laughed. "With news and good advice. Maybe he is not such a bad person after all."

The sisters, under house arrest and forced to stay at home, made the best of their situation. When it seemed certain that Victor was not coming back to reopen his bakery, Galina suggested that they open a simple restaurant downstairs, where Lilia could use Victor's kitchen to prepare homemade soups and breads for lunch, served with her specially flavored tea or coffee. Lilia, mourning the loss of her husband, had to be convinced that Galina's plan would be best for them: a small café would provide some income and give them both something to do while they served out their sentences.

But this is not what I want to do, Galina thought to herself as she waited on customers wearing a smile and one of Lilia's frilly aprons over her own plain skirts and sweaters. Whenever she'd see an interesting face in the restaurant or outside on the street, instinctively she'd reach for her camera that was no longer there. All her equipment had been confiscated when she lost her job and she had no money to replace it, but she was determined to start over, and someday to decorate the tiny restaurant with photographs she'd made herself. Perhaps she could sell some of them; she knew she could make beautiful portraits for their customers. Perhaps eventually they could even subdivide the downstairs space, as Soviets often did, turning one business into two; she'd open her own photography studio where she'd set her customers in front of fanciful backdrops she and Lilia would create: an evergreen forest, a sun-drenched meadow filled with wildflowers, a cozy room with a roaring fire, a night sky filled with brilliant stars.

Lilia, more realistic than her sister, did not think about the future, but busied herself inventing new recipes and sewing curtains and matching tablecloths for the restaurant; she was determined to make a success of it. Eventually life in the neighborhood seemed close to normal again. Their deceitful neighbor, Boris Petrov, stopped by each morning. Each time Lilia was kind enough to offer him tea, but he always declined. He was a busy man, he said, tapping a nervous finger on the counter; he must get on with his day. Both women had to sign a document he prepared for them daily, restating their loyalty to the Soviet government.

The kind neighborhood priest also visited, and Lilia invited him to have all his noonday meals in the restaurant. Galina watched the priest closely during his visits; he greeted her warmly when he arrived, but soon he fixed his eyes on Lilia, whose smiles and easy conversation seemed to please him even more than the home-cooked meals she shared with him. Galina marveled at the deep bond they'd developed, in spite of her sister's marriage to Victor and the priest's devotion to God.

"It seems my sister and the priest are in love," she mused privately, wondering whether she'd eventually have to share the upstairs apartment with the two of them, as she'd once shared it with Lilia and Victor.

"I *know*," Galina once whispered to him as he was leaving their café, but her cautious smile told him she'd never interfere with the feelings he and her sister had for each other.

The priest, grateful that so much good fortune had come his way, prayed silently before each meal, not only for the bowl of soup he was about to enjoy, but also that he'd be a proper priest in Lilia's presence, not the good-hearted but errant cowboy he sometimes still yearned to be.

He never told the sisters that it was he, not Victor, who'd put messages in the treats he'd delivered to them in prison. There are some things priests must confess only to the Lord, and then must try hard to forget.

Epilogue

I'm awake now. I just turned around and nipped my own tail to be sure, then let it go and chased it around and around, just because I felt like it.

All of it really happened to me: everything I've told you about, and then some.

I've moved into my new neighborhood. Not the cramped, stuffy box that eventually returned to Earth without me, catching fire and burning to cinders on its way, but the more glorious, expansive place I'd watched from its porthole. Sometimes I travel with the stars, sometimes I follow the sun on its rounds, sometimes I float independently of them all. I'm timeless now; I live everywhere all at once, stretching, romping and rolling over as I please, finally confident this will all last forever.

I don't remember leaping out of my box, but I have several notions about how it might have happened. Sometimes I think I was caught up in one of the prayers I know the kind priest offered in my name. Sometimes I think the red light released me when its glow finally ceased, sacrificing itself to insure my survival. Sometimes I believe I went to sleep and never woke up, but if this is a dream, there's no reason to interrupt it. Most often I'm convinced that Gazenko worked some human magic from down below. I know for a fact that he has kept his promise, that he thinks of me daily, as I think of him.

He did a nice thing for Albina after they got back to the kennel. She missed me so much that he decided to find new friends for her to frolic with. He tied a red ribbon around her neck and sent her in a car with his assistant, Korinna the Poodle Girl, to a house in my old neighborhood where two sisters lived. Korinna carried Albina in her arms to the front door and knocked. When a woman with mussed red hair answered the door, she and Korinna acknowledged each other with small smiles, and then Korinna transferred Albina to the red-haired woman's arms, saying simply, "For your sister."

Mushka, I'm sorry to report, died on a later mission, when her box tried to bring her home, but veered off course instead, and just before landing on foreign soil, *exploded for no apparent reason*. At least she got to float briefly among the stars. Eventually the scientists got it right; two new kennel dogs, Belka and Strelka, flew on another Sputnik for a long time and then floated safely back home. Strelka had babies after that; one of her puppies traveled to America when our leader Khrushchev gave her to the new American leader Kennedy — he had two children who'd play with the puppy.

I wonder if that puppy ever found out what happened to her mother and to her mother's traveling partner: both Belka and Strelka, after they died, were stuffed and put on display in the Soviet space museum. When I found out about this, I was happy indeed that I'd never returned home, and that I'd never had to suffer such indignities. Humans are so needy about preserving themselves and their history, and they have unusual methods for doing this.

Their history has been kind enough to me, however. I was named a true Soviet hero. A small plaque honoring my exemplary work was put up at the Institute where I'd once lived, and later I showed up in a statue commemorating all fallen cosmonauts; I'm there now, in Star City, peeking out from behind someone's space boot. There were lesser honors as well: postage stamps and candy tins and cigarettes with my picture on them; even a brand of vodka was named after me.

The love of my short little life, Gazneko, his place in Soviet space history assured, went back to work, but soon left the kennel and stopped training dogs in order to prepare humans to fly into space — he seemed to think of this as a promotion. He trained the first human, Yuri Gagarin, to get into a box not much bigger than the one in which I'd traveled. They lit a fire underneath and sent him into the sky; his trip lasted less than two hours, but the way they celebrated when he returned, you'd think he'd been away for a lifetime. Then they sent more men and women, singly like me, then in pairs and eventually they established small communities there in bigger boxes called space stations, and soon men and women from America and other countries joined this community and lived in the boxes alongside the Soviets, now called Russians (the Soviet Union had somehow disappeared from the blanket that still rotates beneath me).

The Chief Designer kept to his hectic schedule, always designing the next spacecraft even before the current one was launched, and more powerful missiles that sent some of his satellites all the way to the moon. He was working on his next design, a spacecraft that would take humans to the moon, when suddenly he died, some said from injuries he'd sustained long ago while in the gulag.

The next day his identity was revealed to the world; at last his incredible contributions to the Soviet space program were acknowledged. Finally his daughter found out what her father did for a living. In a very public ceremony the very, very important Sergei Pavlovich Korolev was buried with full honors, wearing all his medals, inside the Kremlin walls.

Khrushchev, the human who'd been in such an absolute rush to get the Soviets into space, was named "Man of the Year" by an American magazine, and they put his big happy face on the cover. No one mentioned what he'd done to me; no one mentioned me at all after a while, and eventually even most of the folks who'd known about me forgot about my unprecedented sacrifice. Today, only a handful of humans remember who I am and what I did, but I cannot waste my afterlife fretting over that.

I am too busy here, marking my territory, because there is no end to this place. It goes on forever. Every time I turn around, I find some new boundary I've never seen before, and must hurry past it, then squat and pee. Gazenko was right; until we test the boundaries, we cannot know what lies beyond.

No number of satellites in orbit, footsteps on the moon, or space probes to distant planets will ever change the fact that I was here first, all of it accented by small markers I've deposited everywhere. If you ever travel into space yourself, no doubt you'll recognize my scent, and you'll know this place belongs to me.

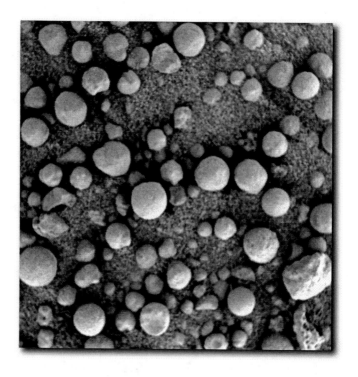

A patch of soil on Mars, examined by the Mars Exploration Rover Opportunity, was unofficially named "Laika" by NASA mission controllers. (Photo: NASA)

Acknowledgements

Many thanks to Dale Alan Bailes, my excellent editor, faithful friend and longtime supporter of my artistic impulses, whatever they have been.

Thanks to my friend and color matching guru Howard Simkins, who helped me get my RGB head around CMYK, ensuring that the colors on my book cover would look as glorious in print as they look on my computer monitor.

Special thanks to Chris Dubbs, space dog specialist extraordinaire, who was always ready to answer questions and share information. Chris was especially helpful in tracking down photos, as was Francois Vig. Thanks to Topps for permission to use a vintage bubblegum card as my cover art, and to Jill Newmark at the National Medical Library, who provided the high-reslolution image.

Thanks also to Mary Ann Rogoff, who read and commented on an early draft, and to Lucy Baringolts, Andy Padlo and Elena Bukareva, who helped with specifics of Russian wording.

Maternal thanks to my son Woody for growing up nicely, so I now can spend less time worrying and more time writing.

Exceptional and ongoing thanks to my husband Phill Sawyer, always ready to help me dream big.

About the Author

Jan Millsapps is a versatile and accomplished writer whose work truly exemplifies the digital age; she has produced films, videos, digital and interactive cinema, and has published traditional print and online media. She is a featured blogger on Apple's Learning Interchange and contributing editor for the online, rich media journal "Academic Intersections."

Her films have been shown at the Smithsonian Institute, Kennedy Center, the International Center of Photography in New York, and the De Young Museum in San Francisco, and her multimedia work has been featured at the National Educational Film and Video Festival, the Mill Valley Film Festival, San Francisco City Hall and USC's Interactive Frictions Conference.

Her scholarly articles, political and personal essays, poetry and short stories have appeared in the *San Francisco Chronicle*, the *San Francisco Examiner*, on *The New York Times* wire service, in *The State Magazine* and in *Film/Literature Quarterly*.

She holds a Ph.D. in composition and rhetoric and recently earned a certificate in cosmology. She lives in San Francisco where she teaches screenwriting and digital cinema courses at San Francisco State University and water aerobics at the YMCA.